Under the
Mandarin Tree

Agnese Mulligan

First published in the UK in 2021

ISBN 9798780129899

Typesetting and ebook production by Laura Kincaid,
Ten Thousand | Editing + Book Design
www.tenthousand.co.uk

Printed by Amazon

To my wonderful mother

Contents

Thanks

To my husband Mark who supported me throughout the writing of this book and with the historical research.

Thank you also to my friend Debora with whom I started this journey back in 2014. Her help, knowledge and experience of the writing process was invaluable. Together we spent many memorable writing weekends. In between a cocktail and a nice evening meal, we would immerse ourselves in our Sicilian origins and talk about our shared experience of being Sicilians living in England. It was a perfect blend of hard work and laughter.

To Signor Franco La Pica for the precious time he spent helping me understand what life was like in Taormina during and after the war. Signor Franco left us before I finished this book but I will be always grateful for his help. His absolute love and passion for '*la sua* Taormina' – his Taormina – will never be forgotten.

Thank you to all the people who, over the years, pushed me to write this book – you know who you are.

My final thanks go to you, Sicily. We have had our differences, but you will always be my home and heart. You are a land of passion, intense flavours, troubled histories, shimmering heat, a confluence of cultures. You can instil frustration and longing in me in the same moment. You are a land of contradictions, highs and lows, successes and failures. But in you I will always see my truest self.

Prologue

It would be impossible to count how many times I've been told that I should write a book about my family history. Nor indeed how many times I've smiled and murmured, 'One day…' in polite reply.

I was born Beatrice Curcurace and it's a name that defines both my life and my Sicilian heritage. In English, 'Beatrice' is simply pronounced 'Bee-a-triss', but in Italian the name is the distinctly more glamorous sounding 'Bay-a-tree-cha'. It's not a pronunciation that is either immediately obvious or natural to the English, and first introductions almost always involve me giving a short lesson in Italian phonetics.

To make things worse, my surname isn't exactly an easy one to say either, and I usually end up spelling it out for people: C-U-R-C-U-R-A-C-E. It comes from the area of Taormina – my home town – and it originally referred to people coming from the nearby village of Curcuraci. Curcuraci and Taormina are situated in the province of Messina, which itself sits on Sicily's east coast, an area rich in both the Arabic and Greek influences with which Sicily is imbued.

I left Sicily almost thirty years ago, in my early twenties, and came to England. When I arrived, I didn't mind people opting for the English Beatrice rather than struggling with the Italian *Beatrice*. That was until a work colleague explained that in England no one under the age of eighty is called Beatrice, unless they're either a princess or pretentious. From then on, I stuck to my real name, pronounced the Italian way. Even today

I still appreciate it when people make the effort to try to pronounce it correctly. Sometimes they get it right and sometimes they don't, but at least they try.

When my parents decided to call me Beatrice more than fifty years ago, they wouldn't have imagined I would end up living in England, the native land of the high-born woman I was named after: Beatrix Howard. Beatrix had died long before I was born and her mother had also been called Beatrix, so the origins of my name stretch far back into the depths of the nineteenth century. But why would my lowly born Sicilian parents name me after a well-to-do English lady? For most of my life I'd simply assumed that it had something to do with the fact they'd named my brother Edoardo after Mr Edward Cecil Page, an aristocratic Englishman living in Taormina. Then, some years ago, I found myself with reason to start questioning my parents' motivation, and before long I knew that the day had finally come for me to write my book.

1

The Awakening

'Interesting photo,' my husband Richard remarked on his way through the dining room on a wide-eyed tour of my father's elegant Sicilian home, the hidden gem that is Villa Sole in the ancient hilltop town of Taormina.

'Oh yes. It's by the famous German photographer Wilhelm von Gloeden,' I replied, trotting behind him, eager to impress with my cultural knowledge. 'Edward Cecil Page was a collector. Remember, I told you he was the one who gave this house to my father?'

Richard stood for a little longer, taking in the naked black-and-white torso of a young boy in an ancient Greek pose, complete with the obligatory laurel wreath crown symbolising leadership.

'These photos have been here ever since I can remember,' I continued. 'Now, shall we stay in or go out for dinner?'

He paused in front of the photo, his back to me, before replying, 'Let's go out.' I could tell his mind was already racing with questions about the eccentric house.

After years of estrangement, I was visiting my father Francesco – or 'Ciccio' as he had been known for most of his life – and his second wife Petronilla. Villa Sole was his home and had once been mine also. For the first time ever, I was there with my own family: Richard, myself and our big brown-eyed, rosy-cheeked eight-month-old daughter Erica. We had named her after her great-grandfather Eric. I was knotted with anxiety, hoping for the trip to be a roaring success despite it being threatened by more complications than I would have cared to imagine. Every family has its problems, but mine more than most.

I'd put off this visit for years, but now felt like the right time. Maybe proud new motherhood had softened me, or maybe I simply wanted to repay Richard some of the generous hospitality that his own warm, loving English family had lavished on me since we'd gone from being merely office colleagues to a couple. Whatever the reason, I wanted to put old grievances aside for the sake of my husband and child.

It wasn't easy to do though. The past couldn't be changed, and I was never going to condone my father's behaviour. He'd fractured my childhood, leaving our home at the start of every week to live another life with another person in another city. It was a life in which my brother, my mother and I played no part and knew little of. Then he would return at the weekend as if it was just a normal routine. He didn't notice – and if he did, he didn't care – that as every Monday came around, my mother Linetta's heart would break a little more, her dedication and affection discarded at the end of the weekend. Eventually, after my mother passed away, my father remarried, and now here we all were.

The visit had got off to a good enough start as soon as we'd pulled into the gravel drive in the hire car from the airport. My father, sitting smoking under the mandarin tree in the courtyard, immediately stood up and greeted us both warmly in the traditional Italian way, with a kiss on each cheek. Anyone who'd met my father always said what a lovely man he was. Charismatic with a capital C. Perhaps that was his downfall. Within no time though, Petronilla appeared, kissing us both and making a huge fuss of Erica as we all drank coffee and discussed sleeping arrangements.

'This is stunning!' Richard said, clearly agog at the surroundings. 'I know you've described it to me, but I didn't expect it to be quite like this – it's just amazing.'

Having grown up in Villa Sole, I perhaps didn't always appreciate quite how spectacular it was. With its well-preserved Roman walls bursting with history and lush gardens filled with banana, citrus and fig trees, nobody can visit Villa Sole and not be impressed by its beauty – or struck by its peaceful tranquillity, despite being only a few hundred metres away from Taormina's lively historical centre.

After we settled down in the bedroom that used to be my parents' and Erica had had a little nap, we went out.

'*Ciao, Beatrice, come stai?* – Hi, Beatrice, how are you?' an old family friend called over to us during our *passeggiata sul* Corso Umberto, a stroll along the main street of Taormina.

The *passeggiata* plays an important role in Sicilian culture. Usually taken before dinner, everyone dresses smartly, children included, and goes out for a leisurely walk, talking with friends and acquaintances along the way. In a small place like Taormina, a short distance that could otherwise be walked in ten minutes can take up to an hour, becoming a long series of interruptions, greetings and small talk.

Corso Umberto lies at the heart of Taormina, running across the old town. The town itself is set within Roman walls, and at either end of Corso Umberto are two gateways – Porta Catania and Porta Messina. These used to be the town's southern and northern entrances, one facing towards the city of Catania and the other north, towards Messina. Over the centuries, Taormina's walls have repelled invaders as diverse as Arabs, Normans and Spanish.

What makes the process of the *passeggiata* so fascinating and spectacularly beautiful is the vivid confusion of colours, smells, sights and sounds. The Corso is a potted history of Taormina's complex past, a resplendent mix of medieval, Gothic and even Roman architecture, each era calling out for recognition.

Ancient stonework juts out between stylish luxury shops selling antiques, designer clothes and high-end jewellery, all jostling for attention among endless racks of cheap tourist T-shirts and knick-knacks.

Squeezed between Tower of Pisa souvenirs and plastic donkeys, regimented rows of polished Mussolini busts carved out of volcanic rock from Mount Etna stare defiantly at the slow-moving mass of people. Elsewhere, vibrant craft-shop window displays contain row upon row of the characteristic blue-and-yellow Sicilian Caltagirone pottery. Many shops also have intricate handmade crochet pieces, like those my mother and aunt had made for my dowry, *la dote*. Above the endless sea of heads, balconies overflow with an immense variety of fragrant flowers, and rooftop restaurants resonate with the clinking of wine glasses.

The Corso is Taormina's main artery, off which lead countless narrow, winding streets that creep up towards the mountains, while others cascade down towards the distant sea. Hidden in each little side street, small cafes and shops compete for the incessant flow of passing trade.

With such a bewildering assault on the senses, there was little chance for Richard to get bored during our long evening *passeggiata*. At every stop he smiled patiently, making polite conversation and then waiting for me while I repeated the same script over and over again: 'I'm OK, thank you. *Come va?* – How's it going? We're here on holiday. This is my husband,' and so on.

'Shall we go for an aperitif?' Richard asked. I knew he was secretly hoping that nobody I knew would sit next to us, his mind still full from before. Unfortunately, that proved to be difficult. As we went into a bar opposite the main piazza and sat down, a voice came from the neighbouring table.

'Beatrice, *bentornata! Come stai?* – Beatrice, welcome back! How are you?'

Poor Richard! His face wore a patiently resigned look but he continued to smile, knowing how important this annual trip home was for me. Nevertheless, it continued to amaze him just how many people I still knew in Taormina.

Eventually we were alone with our drinks and sat back to watch the sky turn red with the setting sun. Mount Etna, the vast volcano that looms over the whole of the south-eastern end of Sicily, was sleepily bubbling red lava down its side while the deep blue sea down below glittered with the last glimmers of sunlight. Erica was asleep in her pushchair and I looked at her in complete awe, wondering how I'd produced such a beautiful creature. A happy, good-natured child, Erica is a true blend of her British and Italian heritage. Her flawless English-rose skin is the perfect backdrop for her dark, almost black eyes. Smiling, I sat back in my chair, drinking in the intoxicating scene. The moment was perfection, everything in its place and all well in our world.

I turned to Richard and said with an encouraging smile, 'Let's find a quiet place for dinner,' while wracking my brain to think of a restaurant where no one was likely to know me. We ventured into one of the tiny side streets off the Corso and found an *osteria* called Don Carmelo. I was pleasantly surprised to discover a charming little place that I didn't even know existed. Richard, though, looked sceptical, but he smiled and said, 'Well, it looks nice. Let's go in.'

At first glance, the place was empty – not a good sign – but then we realised that it was still quite early and Italians notoriously eat very late. But it was nice to be just the three of us. The food was simple, with mainly Sicilian specialties on the menu. Richard is vegetarian, but luckily Sicily is a vegetarian's paradise, with so many different tasty vegetable dishes, such as *pasta al forno vegetariana* (baked vegetarian pasta), *caponata* (a vegetable ratatouille), *peperonata* (a pepper-based dish), *parmigiana* (baked aubergines)… The list is endless.

'This *cipollata* is just to die for,' I said as I bit into a delicious tuna chunk cooked with sweet and sour onions, something I hadn't eaten in years. The smell instantly took me back to dinnertime at Zio Ruggero's terrace. Nobody made *cipollata* like Zio Ruggero.

'Nero d'Avola, *per favore*.' Richard said after choosing the wine. During our trip, Nero d'Avola would become one of his favourites. This delicious red is named after Avola, a small town in south-east Sicily where growers selected the grape variety several hundred years ago.

'So…' Richard began, taking in the aroma of the dark wine in his glass, 'the house. Tell me again. How did your dad get it? Did he live there?'

'Well…' I said, trying to recall memories of my past. 'My dad was adopted by an English aristocrat, and upon his death, he left him all his money.'

'Adopted?' Richard asked curiously. 'So, this aristocrat didn't marry or have any relatives back in England? Why did your grandmother give him up for adoption? How old was he?'

It was while trying to answer his many questions that I realised I didn't actually have the answers, and I was instantly surprised that I'd never actively looked for any beforehand. Embarrassed by my lack of information about my own family history, I began to feel uncomfortable and irritated.

'No, he never married and didn't have any direct relatives!' I said somewhat snappily.

'*Ecco la sua pasta alla Norma, Signore. Buon appetito!*'

Richard's main course arrived – pasta with fried aubergines, tomato sauce and smoked, salted ricotta – and I felt relieved and hopeful that he would now concentrate on his meal rather than on interrogating me. The smell of the food seemed to have awoken Erica so I picked her up, another welcome distraction.

As Richard ate, thoughts cascaded through my mind. I needed to gather more information, or just come clean and admit that in actual fact I didn't know much about my family history at all.

Before we were ready to leave, the owner brought us a complementary *limoncello*, a liqueur made from lemon zest, and also some *cannoli Siciliani*, tube-shaped shells made of fried pastry dough with a sweet, creamy filling usually consisting of ricotta and dried fruit. We couldn't refuse such a generous offer. Later, the owner told us that he knew my mother. *Una gran bella signora* – a really beautiful lady, he said.

As we strolled back towards Villa Sole, the air had cooled a little and the Corso Umberto was quieter than it had been earlier in the afternoon. Different melodies drifted from the numerous bars and cafes: a live jazz band, a group playing the *tarantella* (a lively southern Italian folk dance) and a solo piano player singing 'Strangers in the Night'. Soon, we arrived at the piazza, and all the different music, mixed with the laughter and shouting of kids running around, created a chaotic sound, so familiar to me but strange to Richard's ears.

'Do kids ever go to bed here?' he asked, smiling at the sight of dozens of young children running around and having fun as if it was the middle of the day.

'Not until the parents do!' I replied.

Back at the villa, while fetching a glass of water from the kitchen, I paused in front of the von Gloeden photograph. I stared at it for a few minutes but with different eyes now and with so many new, answerless questions running through my mind. *Why was the young boy in the photo close to naked? If my father was adopted, then why was my maiden name Curcurace and not Cecil Page?*

I looked around, taking in the house I'd grown up in, all the familiar objects, furniture and paintings, and for the first time I saw everything differently. More questions, more doubts, and the uncomfortable sense that things weren't quite as they'd always seemed crept into my mind.

It was then and there that I decided: *I want to know more. I need to know more.* And so my search for the truth began.

2

Another 'Lucky One' Arrives

Maria Greco
(Head cook at Villa Sole. October 1946)

It is 4 p.m. on the dot and I am preparing sardines to grill for my employer Signor Edoardo's dinner when a skinny, scruffy little boy suddenly runs barefooted and laughing into my kitchen. My daughters Mena and Linetta must have let him in. I can hear them playing in the garden.

Tonight, Signor Edoardo will be joined by a very important literary guest – Mr Truman Capote. On his frequent visits here, he has often been effusive in his praise for my fresh, traditional cuisine, so I'd better finish peeling the potatoes before putting the chickpeas in water to make *pastelle di ceci* – chickpea batter – later on. While I would shrug off his compliments, I'm secretly happy to please. It keeps me in work here as sole cook – and in this poverty-stricken village, jobs aren't easy to come by. My husband Beppe is the gardener too, so we are truly blessed.

Signor Edoardo is known locally as 'the Baron', a term used to refer to many of the foreigners residing in Taormina. He's a good man and looks after us well. Tonight, for instance, as it's a special day for everyone when he entertains, so much food will be prepared that inevitably there will be leftovers to take home, with his approval. I'm already thinking about the delicious fish soup I'll make with all the sardines' heads and bones. What a treat.

Through all his travels, Signor Edoardo has acquired a very sophisticated palate, but luckily for me he prefers the most simple and genuine food the land has to offer. Anything grown under the fierce Sicilian sun and fished out of the deep blue sea is acceptable to him, and he has no wish for anything else.

I was informed of the child's imminent arrival by Venera the housekeeper just after I'd served Signor Edoardo his lunch, which he ate in the courtyard under the cool shade of the mandarin tree. He was sleepy after his meal – three slices of mature goat's cheese and a slice of homemade sourdough bread with a salad of big fresh basil leaves fetched by Mena and Linetta, plump tomatoes from the garden and red onions marinated in lemon and vinegar, a pinch of sea salt and a splash of extra virgin olive oil from the Olive Yard in Mufabbi. *Perfetto!* Perfect!

After washing it all down with Bass beer sent from his native England, Signor Edoardo was ready for a *riposino* – afternoon nap. But before he retired to his room, I was told that I must welcome this boy, Francesco, and his mother, Concetta. They must be instructed to wait in the courtyard until he reappears.

I played dumb, but as a local I already knew all about little Francesco – or 'Ciccio' as he's affectionately called by his family and friends, including myself. He's the youngest of his widowed mother's eight children. Everyone in Taormina knows each other's business. Especially something as important and life-changing as this… Going into the 'Baron's House' has been the answer to many a poor family's prayers in these parts. One less mouth to feed. And boys – they always seem to be young boys that Signor Edoardo takes in – are always hungry. Willing workers with empty stomachs. Little Ciccio proved to be no different.

Once the smiling introductions are out of the way, I direct Ciccio and his mother: 'Signor Edoardo said to wait in the courtyard. *Sittativi e aspittati* – sit down and wait please.'

I pour freshly squeezed orange juice into two glasses, put two almond cakes on a plate and ask Mena to give it to them, annoying her younger sister in the process.

Within seconds, Ciccio has greedily devoured the drink and cake as an embarrassed Concetta scolds him to slow down and be polite. Poor mite, this is probably the only thing he's eaten all day. The same would be true of the others at home. When her husband Ignazio, the village baker, passed away after a long illness, Concetta was left with all eight children to support, as well as her mother-in-law, who lived with them in such bleak conditions. The poor woman had already buried her eldest son, too weak and fragile to survive the post-war poverty and struggles after the loss of his father. God forbid it should happen again. I prepared a little bag with bread, cheese, olives and milk for her to take away.

But today Concetta must feel as if God is finally listening to her desperate prayers. From this moment on, Ciccio's life and the life of all his family will change for the better with Signor Edoardo's kindness and support. Just as it did for me and my family. This handsome but malnourished-looking boy of ten or eleven who sits before me in a torn, faded shirt and ragged trousers that are far too small, and probably passed down from all his brothers, is about to step into a whole new blessed life. One of the lucky ones.

3

A Special Place

With our family trip to Sicily long behind us, we'd moved into our beautiful new hilltop home in Lancashire. I woke to the sound of incessant rain streaming down the bedroom window and on a whim, I decided to stay indoors rather than brave the wet, grey day to do the weekly grocery shop.

'What a miserable morning,' I said with a shiver. Although it was July, it hadn't stopped raining for more than a week and there was a permanent chill in the air.

I forced myself out of bed and then into warmer clothes than the season should have dictated. Staring absent-mindedly out of my bedroom window, I found myself thinking about Signor Edoardo again – he'd been on my mind ever since we'd returned from Sicily months earlier. He'd been troubling me, to be honest. Richard opened a can with his questions and worms were now everywhere I looked! I found myself with far more questions than I did answers.

The rain continued to fall in sheets. I doubted I would ever adjust to the English weather, even after calling England home for almost thirty years. Relocating from London to the even wetter Ribble Valley in the north-west to be closer to Richard's parents didn't exactly improve my opinion of the English climate, but moving close to Richard's parents was the most important thing.

After visiting my father, we'd realised just how important blood ties were to us both, and we wanted our own daughter to grow up surrounded by a loving, extended family. A bit of grandparental babysitting now and then wouldn't go amiss either. Nor indeed would the slower pace of life in the countryside. The noise and grime of London were behind me and something I had no desire to return to, so the too-often-dreary weather was a price I was willing to pay. Not that that stopped me complaining though.

'They call this summer!' I grumbled to myself as I walked down the stairs, my thoughts inevitably returning to sun-kissed Sicily, where summers are really summers, with temperatures typically creeping up to 40 degrees. In that moment, how I wished I was there.

I remembered with fondness Sicilian summer mornings, a world away, a life away from the damp green hills around me. It was only since leaving Sicily that I truly appreciated what an idyllic, magical place Villa Sole was to wake up in for a little girl. I could wander straight out onto my bedroom balcony and pick a fat, juicy orange from the tree below. No such luck for Erica sadly. As beautiful as our farmhouse was, with its rolling views of the Lancashire countryside, it couldn't really compare. Her morning juice comes from a shop-bought plastic bottle. Still, at least she could see lambs gambolling in the fields from her bedroom window, so there were compensations and experiences that I never had. Many, in fact.

I'd like to say that my childhood was full of love and happiness, but though there was much love, unfortunately there was also much drama and trauma. I wasn't actually born in Villa Sole itself but in a house nearby, opposite the north entrance of the villa. This was the house where my parents went to live after they married, gifted to them by Signor Edoardo.

Looking back, I realised quite how much I loved that house. It was light, airy and modern, with a fantastic view of the sea,

Mount Etna and the mountains behind. With hindsight I could see that this was the house where I'd experienced the happiest moments of my childhood.

While we lived there, we were still well off, and even had a summer residence, Villa Simeto, where we would spend the holidays. It was just ten minutes from Taormina, down in Villagonia by the seaside. We would relocate there as soon as school ended for the summer break, usually around June, and we stayed there until school reopened in late September.

Villa Simeto was a beautiful eight-bedroom house, surrounded by countryside and rich vegetation – mostly citrus trees – and with its own swimming pool. We'd have many guests stay with us, some of them all summer. There was a French lady, Seraphine, my mother's friend, who came many times, sometimes with her family. I still have fond memories of her greeting me after my first day at primary school with an enormous cone filled with sweets and treats, in the traditional French style. I even remember a few French songs that she taught me, songs that I would then sing to Erica. I also remember my godfather with his partner and friends, one of them a Tunisian called Akim whom I adored. These interesting guests seemed to me glamorous, beautiful and successful.

In the seventies, my father, in partnership with some friends, transformed Villa Simeto into a nightclub called Moonlight. During the day it was our summer residence, but every night it would turn into a glittering venue. Very soon, Moonlight became a famous and very exclusive club. People came from all over Sicily and the rest of Italy to see the famous singers and groups that would perform there. There are photographs of eight-year-old me with Italian celebrities of the seventies: I Pooh, Renato Zero, Patty Pravo, I Vianella, Sammy Barbot and many others. I had the best time ever, peeping out of my window or sneaking around when I was supposed to be in bed, or hiding in the DJ's booth with Luca, a family friend. But the greatest fun was the day after a big night.

One of Moonlight's attractions was a retractable glass dance floor built over the swimming pool. The guests looked as if they were dancing on water. Very often at the end of the night, it would be retracted and people would jump into the pool for a drunken swim. The tipsy women would inevitably lose jewellery, and I used to love donning my goggles and flippers to dive in and retrieve lost gems the following morning. Sadly though, I was never allowed to keep my precious catch.

Up until that point in my life, my mother was my anchor and also the one who kept my family together. She was a strong, clever woman who, despite years of suffering, still had a beautiful smile. Even though we were for a long period one of the richest families in Taormina – and possibly Sicily – my mother remained humble and down to earth. Everyone loved her. She instilled values in myself and my brother Edoardo that have thankfully stayed with us throughout our lives. She enjoyed making clothes for me, was an excellent cook, and a proud housewife and hostess. But above all else, she was our mother who loved us unconditionally. Just as I love Erica, and just as I knew I would love her little brother or sister, who I was by then carrying.

Part of me was hoping for a son, for Richard, but also because my mother's siblings each had a boy and a girl. As I was the last of my cousins to have children, part of me wanted to maintain the family tradition, but it really wasn't that important. Son or daughter, the child would be welcomed with open arms, loved and protected by me, always. Is that not what every mother does? Fathers, in my own personal experience, Richard firmly excluded, are a rather different proposition though.

4
Thanks Be to God

Concetta Curcurace
(Widow and mother of eight, October 1916)

Tonight, I shall sleep like a baby. And when I wake tomorrow in this dark, airless room of sweating, hungry bodies, there will be one less mouth to feed. One less little bony body to clothe. Thanks be to God, Ciccio has escaped! He's exchanged this squalor and perpetual hunger for a life you and I could never have dreamed of, Ignazio, for him or any of his four older brothers and three sisters... and then there was Pancrazio, who, weak through malnourishment, joined you in the earth two years after you left us, my dear husband. Me and our precious *'picciriddi'* – kids – left alone to fend for ourselves without you. I feared that Ciccio would be the next to join you both. His limbs are so much scrawnier than even you will remember them.

You always knew that life would not be easy when you left us, didn't you? 'How will you manage?' were among your last weary words to me. Throughout your illness, you watched help-lessly as I battled to try and keep them nourished – and alive – after you stopped bringing home bread from the bakery. I did my best, but I failed Pancrazio. I prayed to San Pancrazio, our town's beloved patron saint, night and day but without success. It breaks my heart every single day.

I tried to grow a few chickpeas and beans on that small patch of dry land we claimed. I still do. But some days there's nothing at all to pick under this scorching sun. So I had nothing to feed us all except for a few leftover crumbs begged from your pitying successor at the bakery and *ficalinni*, prickly pears, picked from the roadside, just like the ones your own mother sold there for *poche lire* – a pittance.

She's still here, and I do my best to keep her with us, but she's failing fast. I don't think she ever got used to losing you and Pancrazio. She believes God should have taken her instead. Maybe she's right. But that isn't our choice to make, is it? We can't dwell on what should have or could have been. We have to look to the future. It's the only way to survive, fortified by our faith and what hope we can muster.

Today, hope arrived for the first time since you left us, Ignazio. Soon now, Ciccio's skinny little body will begin to fatten up and grow stronger. Also, we are reaping a little of the kindness shown to him by Signor Edoardo. He has remunerated me generously for the transaction and there is the promise of a few regular food parcels that will be a godsend. What this place would do without that kind English gentleman and his rich famous guests who arrive to spread their generosity too, I really don't know. I thank God for our benevolent Baron every day.

It all happened so completely by chance. You remember how Ciccio loved playing in the streets with his brothers and friends? Some nights you had to go out in the dark and look for him to bring him home. Well, apparently, he spotted Signor Edoardo walking down the street near the cathedral one day and the elegant old gentlemen must have intrigued him with his fancy dress and air of aristocracy. So much so that he would follow him all the way to Villa Sole, pretending to swing his own imaginary ivory walking cane just as Signor Edoardo did.

This must have really tickled the old man. After all, you know how cheekily charming and mischievous our handsome little devil can be! He began asking his housekeeper to give Ciccio a few jobs, for a glass of milk or a slice of bread and jam. Maybe a piece of fruit or almond cake.

He must have worked hard for it because, out of the blue, when I was tending the vegetable patch one day, I was approached by Signor Edoardo. He asked if I would consider the possibility of Ciccio moving into Villa Sole to join his staff full-time as his permanent aid and companion. Consider! Would I consider?

'Well, if you want to take another three or four of my children to feed and live in your house, you're welcome,' I replied. How could I ever hope to give any of our children the luxurious life that he could provide? Climbing into a comfortable bed with a full belly every night, instead of lying on a cramped stone floor forever hungry? How could I refuse that life for any of our children? And all in return for a few honest tasks. A job! We know how few and far between they are around here.

But enough for now, Ignazio, *marito mio*, my husband. It's time to say my grateful prayers and then settle down for the best night's rest I've had in a long time. *Buona notte* – goodnight.

5

A Drama Not of My Making

One abiding memory that's stayed with me and followed me around the world is of me waking up alone in my mother's big bed one morning in the late seventies. All around me, noisy strangers ransacked drawers, wardrobes and the family safe. Strewn across the white linen bedcover on top of me was all of her best jewellery. My inheritance. Beautiful pieces: diamond earrings, chunky gold rings with precious stones, bracelets and necklaces, all glittering in the early morning Sicilian sunshine. At barely ten years old, I found myself at the centre of a police raid, and I was completely, utterly terrified.

As often happened when my errant father was away, I'd sneaked into my mother's warm bed and her reassuring arms during the middle of the night. A sensitive child, my sleep was often interrupted by fevered dreams and imaginings. She was the only one who could ever comfort me. I only hope that I can have the same magical soothing effect on Erica and her baby brother or sister, should they ever need it.

With the biggest heart and the best will in the world though, I know that there's only so far a mother can protect her child from life's slings and arrows. And never was that more evident than on that particular, peculiar morning.

My mother was nowhere to be seen. I had no idea what was happening. Despite my shy nature, I was a dedicated ballerina who loved performing, who was used to dramas, but they had always been of my own making up until now.

I pulled the bedcover tight up to my chest, frozen still as the action continued regardless of me. Men in uniform shouted to each other, completely oblivious to the little girl caught up in something that she could have no comprehension of. Then my mother suddenly appeared in the doorway, still in her long pink cotton nightdress. My saviour!

I stretched out my arms to her, but one look at her pale, stricken face told me something was very, very wrong. A stern-looking police officer tried to stop her from approaching me, but a kinder colleague let her take me. Shrugging, the officer allowed her to scoop me up and take me downstairs, where yet more drama unfolded.

In the kitchen, normally kept so pristine by my typically Italian house-proud mother, all the cupboard doors were swinging on their hinges. Packets of sugar, flour and salt were ripped open and scattered across the table, contents spilling everywhere. Don't ask me how I knew – maybe I'd picked something up from TV or maybe I'd overheard adult conversations I should not have – but I instinctively knew what they were looking for: drugs.

Suddenly, my mother's older sister Zia Mena – Aunt Mena, my other saviour – arrived to rescue me and take me to her house. Although reluctant to leave my distraught mother, I was also anxious to leave this frightening scene and head for a familiar place of safety. Thank heavens for Zia Mena, who'd always been there for my mother after Nonna Maria – Grandma Maria – had died of *tifo* – typhoid.

My own poor mother had also become ill with it soon afterwards. The chances are that she would have died too, had it not been for Signor Edoardo stepping in and paying for her medical care in the nearby city of Catania. His generosity seemed to know no bounds, and it was always remembered with immense gratitude within the family. As long as I can remember, he was revered. Even in Sicily, where we take our saints very seriously indeed, he was practically canonised.

Over the years, my father had many different businesses apart from Moonlight – mainly restaurants and bars. Very often my mother would go to help and that was the best time for me because I could go and have a sleepover at Zia Mena's. I think she loved having me there as much as I loved being there, because my uncle, Zio Ruggero, was First Chef on an American luxury cruiser called *Pacific Princess* – the very one from *The Love Boat* TV series of the seventies and eighties, as a silver-framed photo above the dining-room table shows. He could be travelling around the world for a whole year sometimes. My cousins Mattia and Marianna are both much older than me and were already working or married, so I was a companion for Zia Mena.

In retrospect, I know why I enjoyed staying there so much – it was a happy house! From the moment I stepped inside, I felt relaxed and secure. I loved the fresh, clean smell. My mother and father were both very heavy smokers, but my brother and I hated smoking and neither of us have ever smoked.

I remember waiting for Zio Ruggero to return from one of his trips with as much anticipation and excitement as my cousins. He always brought so many novelties from America and so many presents for everyone, including me. I'll never forget when he came back with a projector and a number of Mickey Mouse movies.

Zio Ruggero was a kind, amazing man. He didn't have a formal education beyond his primary years, but his 'school' became the world and his travels. He was a very skilled craftsman and there was nothing that he couldn't build or fix. He spent thirty years at sea providing for his family while Zia Mena brought up the children and built three homes. When he retired, they lived the rest of their time together, never spending another day apart, in absolute awe of each other. One of the sweetest things I saw and loved about them was that every day, before every meal, they would kiss each other as a sort of thank you for the food they were about to eat.

It is so easy to understand why I loved being there to witness that. Sadly, Zio Ruggero is no longer with us, but what marvellous role models for a happy, loving marriage he and my aunt were. Especially when the same couldn't be said of my own parents' relationship. As an Italian, I don't need to be reminded of the importance of a loving, extended family but there goes another example of how crucial it really is.

On the day of the police raid, after Zia Mena had managed to calm me down as best she could, she spent the next few hours *a coccolarmi* – indulging me. There were lots of cuddles, unlimited TV, homemade pizza and we even made *gelato* – ice cream – for lunch. Then, several anxious hours later, my mother arrived, in a state of absolute desperation, to spend the night there with me. After that, it was all pretty much a blur.

Nobody actually sat me down and explained what had happened because I was too young, and even for my young age I was pretty naive. Looking back, I'd grown up in a bubble. I was never encouraged to play in the street with the other children, though I was always playing outdoors in the fresh air at the seaside, forever making up my own games with imaginary characters for friends. All I really wanted to be was a ballerina, starting lessons at the age of three. I made my debut solo performance at the age of four and apparently, I wasn't at all intimidated about being on stage on my own. According to family legend, I forgot some steps, but rather than freeze in panic, I improvised by making some up and kept going. A true little star!

I loved performing, and somehow, I always won a leading part in school plays. Some classmates and I created a little theatre company, even writing our own material in Sicilian dialect. The plays were comedies about a Sicilian family – parents and two children. I played the old-fashioned *papà* who struggled to cope with his teenage children in modern times. My friend Rosa was the *mamma*, and Ava and my best friend Anna were the teens. We loved performing, and I can vividly remember what an amazing feeling it was to hear the audience's laughter. We also performed in the nursing home near school. What joy we must have brought to those elderly people. I can still recall the fulfilment I felt at the end of every performance.

That carefree, cosseted life couldn't last forever of course, but did it really have to change as abruptly as it did?

Without knowing it at the time, the day of the raid proved to be the start of a very sad ending for Moonlight. It also marked the beginning of the end of our family and its fortune.

My brother Edoardo, who's eight years older than me, had benefited from the rich life we had enjoyed. He had numerous motorbikes and did motocross, competing in regional championships and even winning a couple of trophies. I remember going to see him and his best friend Rocco in action and it was very exciting, until he badly fractured his ankle in an accident. Soon after, his best friend almost lost his life in another accident. That was the end of Edoardo's motocross career. As compensation, his first car was a Golf GTI, so you can imagine how popular he was. All this popularity, unfortunately for him, came to a swift end when we lost almost everything. In many ways, it must have been much harder for him than me. Many of his so-called 'friends' disappeared, and only a few real ones, like Rocco, remained.

My father spent three months in prison. I received a birthday telegram from him, which I kept for years, and it must still be around in a drawer at home somewhere.

The vague reason I was finally given, and from what I remember reading in the newspapers, was that the Mafia wanted my father to pay protection money known as *il pizzo*. He refused to do so, and they planted a huge amount of cocaine in the club before calling the police to tip them off.

I can still remember the sense of relief I felt that at least he wasn't a criminal associated with the Mafia. Eventually my father was released, but obviously it was all over for Moonlight and the glamorous life that went with it. A great deal of our family's assets had to be sold to pay for my father's lawyers, sparking another chapter in our lives. But not, as it turned out, a good chapter, by any stretch of the imagination. The real heartbreak was yet to come.

6
'*I Buttigghi*' – A Happy Memory

Officially it was the eldest of the four siblings, Zia Amalia, who stepped in to become the replacement matriarch, and I remember her with great affection. She was a real extrovert. Very flamboyant, but a wonderful support for my mum, aunt and their brother Zio Totò – Uncle Totò. My memories of her are more as a grandmother to me than an aunt.

It was Zia Mena with whom I formed an incredibly close bond as a young girl, especially so from that point in my life. I always loved going to her house and spending time with her, but there was one day of the year more than any other that I looked forward to going there. Even today, the memories are so vivid that I can practically smell and taste it.

'*Oggi facemu i buttigghi* – today we're making the bottles.' For as long as I can remember, this was the phrase I would wait for with eager anticipation every summer. It was the one day in July where we wouldn't go to the seaside – something we would normally only miss due to illness or extreme weather conditions. But on this particular July day, all of the women in the family would meet at Zia Mena's house to make *passata di pomodoro fresca* – fresh passata tomato sauce – for the winter. My aunts Amalia and Mena, my cousins Lia and Marianna, and my mother and I would get together to create a fun but extremely effective and organised work chain. Three sisters, three daughters and three cousins.

Everyone had their own role and knew exactly what to do – even I, the youngest, from the age of seven. My task was to help wash the tomatoes and, after they'd cooked, blend them. It may not sound like a particularly big job, but Zia Mena would always make me feel that it was essential, a task that required 'care and precision'. I can remember even now just how important and excited the responsibility would make me feel.

We would wake up very early to start while the temperature – which can reach 30 or 40 degrees in July – was still bearable. The aim was to finish by midday.

On arrival, Zia Mena, Zia Amalia and my cousins would be enjoying their morning coffee, chatting away, and my mother would join them. Impatient as ever, I couldn't wait to go to the big terrace and get started on the work. There, centre stage, was an enormous cauldron bubbling away on a wood-fired stove, just like the one witches use in children's storybooks.

Next to the outside laundry sink, a mountain of juicy red San Marzano tomatoes would be piled high in big wooden baskets, ready to be washed. July and August are the months when tomatoes are at their ripest.

To the right of the stove sat big basil plant pots, lined up against the wall, each containing different kinds of basil. Some had small leaves, some big, but all were green and rich in flavour. I can still smell that fragrant, powerful aroma.

Though I didn't know it, the Sicilian sun is the crucial element for such flavoursome ingredients to work with. The red of the tomatoes and the green of the basil were like a vivid painting set against the golden sun, bright blue sky and the Saracen castle perched on top of the mountain that loomed in front of my aunt's house.

It was the day when all of my senses would come alive. After coffee, everyone else came out to the terrace, ready to start. Zia Mena gave me the little apron she'd made for me, which I would use every time we cooked together. We all wore aprons, very light cotton dresses and flip-flops, with bandanas round our heads, ready for it all to get very hot. We were ready to work, even if it never felt like work to me. All I can remember is the laughter and the joy of it.

We would start by washing the tomatoes in small quantities. I enjoyed the feeling of the fresh, cold water running through my hands while holding the firm, ripe tomato. Even though the sun would not yet be high in the sky, the heat from the cauldron would make us all sweat. Lia would splash me with water several times and I loved it.

Once the tomatoes were washed and drained, the grown-ups would put them in the cauldron of boiling water. It was a task that not even Lia and Marianna, then twenty-two and fifteen, were allowed to do, due to the risk of scalding. Their first job was to pick the best basil leaves from the pots, wash them and leave them to dry on the big wooden board that had been made by Zia Mena's husband Zio Ruggero. I would help with picking as well, loving the smell the basil left on my hands.

After the tomatoes had boiled and the skin was much softer and smoother, they would be taken out to be drained in white muslin and manually pressed to get as much water out as possible. This was another job I wasn't allowed to do, as the tomatoes were deemed too hot. Only when the three sisters were satisfied that there was just enough water left would we start putting them through *passa pomodoro* – a special tomato press – where the skin would come out from one side and the blended juicy tomato from the other. I used to imagine that the delicious smell must have reached the far side of Taormina.

At break time, we would swig welcome glasses of fresh lemonade with ice and salt in – a good way to rehydrate after the 'big sweat', as my mother used to call it. The salt would replace the minerals we had lost. I can still taste the refreshing bitter, salty taste. The first sip was always the worst and would made me shiver until I got used it, after which I loved it. Zia Mena would then take out some almond biscuits and plum cake that I would have helped her bake the day before.

I loved listening to the three sisters chatting, gossiping, teasing each other and laughing loudly as we ate. My mother was happy there, as was I. But I would always be trying not to think about the fact that we had to go home at the end of the day. I realise now that my mother would have been doing the same.

I buttigghi was strictly women's work! Even though Zio Ruggero was a chef, his only job on those days would be to empty the boiling water out of the cauldron. While the women worked away, he would be keeping out of the way, pottering around the house doing his little DIY jobs. However, if Zia Mena's son Mattia was around, he would be allowed to stay, as he loved spending time with all the women in the family.

After the break it was time for *l'imbottigliamento* – bottling duties – putting the passata in the previously sterilised bottles using big funnels. The bottles were normally old Birra Messina, local brown beer bottles, but there could be odd-shaped ones too.

Lia and Marianna would line up all the bottles on the tables and surfaces, and once each bottle was filled, we would put three basil leaves in each. Then the lids were put on. The bottles were next placed very carefully alongside each other in the cauldron, with newspaper separating each one to avoid breaking while they simmered in hot water.

So intrigued by these steps, I would always ask questions and wouldn't be satisfied with a simple answer. As I learned, this stage of the process sealed the passata, making it airtight and long-lasting. Despite this, though, I do remember one bottle randomly exploding in the cupboard months later!

The last job was counting the bottles, and with my mother's help we counted two hundred to be equally divided between the three sisters and used throughout winter. We would finish by midday, after which it was time to celebrate with a big lunch made of *maccheroni fatti in casa* – homemade fresh pasta – with *passata di pomodoro fresca*, of course. This was just one of Zia Mena's many specialities that we enjoyed making together.

I don't recall when we stopped making *i buttigghi*, but unfortunately at some stage we did. What I can remember was someone saying, 'We don't need them anymore. You can buy them in the supermarket and they're just as good.'

I never believed it then and no passata has ever tasted so good for me since. The memory of it is as vivid as they come and a poignant reminder that my childhood, for all its overwhelming traumas, wasn't entirely bad, thanks to my mother and her sisters.

7

A Mother Scorned

Donna Sarina Calapitrulli
(Friend of Concetta, wife and mother of four, October 1916)

I'm staring at a pathetically small pile of potatoes and wondering how in God's name I can eke them out to scrape three family suppers together for six hungry people when I'm interrupted by a knock at the door. Glad of the distraction, I open it to find my good friend and neighbour Concetta standing outside. Not like her. She usually knocks and comes straight in.

'Do you know any good conjurers who can do a bit of magic and triple the size of this lot so we don't all starve this week?' I ask her, pointing at the miserable mound fresh from my unproductive vegetable patch.

She laughs and shakes her head. Like me, Concetta knows how impossible it can be to find enough food to go around, especially when you have four ravenous, growing sons to feed. I have never known any other way of life, thanks to the lump of a husband I was foolish enough to marry, but it hasn't always been as bad for Concetta. Ignazio was a good man and a good provider when he was alive and well. Orazio *mio* – my Orazio – could have done with taking a few tips from him. Oh, he can skip his siestas to find odd work helping the fishermen down in Mazzarò Bay when he needs money for playing cards or another bottle of *vino*. But not much of it ever comes my way to put proper food on the table.

I shrug and sigh at Concetta. She's a good friend and I'm lucky to have her there to talk to. There's no use trying to get Orazio to listen to my permanent woes. Daily life with a family to look after is an exhausting chore when you're poor in Taormina, and you need a bit of moral support to lighten your load, psychologically if not always practically.

Walking down to the river and back with a pile of heavy wet washing or a water jug on your head, for instance, doesn't seem quite as far or as back-breaking when there's someone to share the journey with and a little gossip along the way. Today, though, Concetta's looking a bit out of sorts. I wonder what's happened? She hasn't been the same since she lost Pancrazio, but we usually manage to gee each other up. God knows how, but we were both blessed with the same stoicism.

'Something wrong?' I ask, and if I didn't know her better I would say she looked a bit sheepish.

'I've had a bit of good news…'

'Go on!' I prompt, genuinely excited for her. Good news doesn't come along every day in these parts. Perhaps it will even rub off on me.

'Well, you know the Baron was looking to employ a new apprentice up at Villa Sole a few weeks ago?'

'Huh! That's news to me,' I reply, wondering how the hell I missed that one. The last time the Baron was hiring, I spent six hours queuing in the baking heat with Costanzo, hoping he would arrive and employ him on the spot as an errand boy, kitchen help, gardener's mate… whatever was going. Almost all the mothers in the village were doing just the same with their sons. Needs must and all that.

'Well,' she starts again, 'Ciccio has been offered a job there. He moved in yesterday.'

'How?' I ask, still baffled as to how the opportunity completely bypassed my family.

Maybe the Baron would have chosen my Costanzo over Ciccio, had we known. Oh, Ciccio's a handsome boy all right, but he's also got a streak of something unpredictable about him. Costanzo would have been a steadier pair of hands to have around, being nothing like his father. I stare back at the potatoes and sigh again as Concetta starts nervously chattering away.

'It just happened out of the blue. Signor Edoardo approached me and asked if he could take him in. I don't know what he expected me to say. As if I'd refuse! We all know what this means...'

'We do, Concetta.'

We certainly do. Decent plates of food on the table every night, not a measly few grey lumps of potato. And when the employment ends, there is a pension waiting. Full bellies all round, security for life.

I see red, I'm so cross with myself and Concetta and the Baron at this point. As much as I try not to sound as bitterly jealous as I'm feeling, I know I'm failing. Why does she get the luck? Again. Surely, it's my turn for a bit? I know he isn't here anymore, but she had a good husband for years. What have I done wrong?

Seeing the disappointment on my face and no doubt sensing my bitter mood, Concetta looks apologetically at me and I want to slap her. And scream. Very loudly. Oh, the unfairness of it! I listen as she explains the circumstances, how Ciccio had charmed Signor Edoardo and there had never been an employment process as such this time.

'I should have mentioned it earlier, but I wanted to make sure it all went as planned. I didn't want to jinx anything,' she says, adding, 'And it all happened so fast.'

Yes, you bloody well should have, Concetta, I want to yell at her. We're supposed to be friends. We share stuff so we can both survive better. It's what we do. This is nothing short of betrayal of a fellow struggling mother. I am fuming.

'I know it must be disappointing for you after missing out last time,' she says.

Oh, remind me of that, why don't you, Concetta? Yes, I was disappointed that boy from Dietro I Cappuccini was chosen when the head of that family was a carpenter and they only had three children to feed anyway. What did he have that my Costanzo did not?

'I think maybe you should go now,' I tell her. 'I need to get on.'

She raises her eyebrows as if she's about to protest but thinks better of it. Turning around, she opens the door and says she'll see me tomorrow.

'Yes, yes,' I say. 'Goodbye for now.'

Secretly though, I'm wondering if our friendship will ever be the same again after a test like this.

I pick up a knife and two potatoes and, with the precision of a surgeon, start to very thinly peel them to stretch out what little there is.

'Pray tell me, God, please, what is your purpose here?' I beg, because even without these blessed tears ruining my vision, I certainly can't see one.

8

My Poor, Beautiful Mother

My husband's first jaw-dropping impression of my old family home bore absolutely no resemblance to my own, years beforehand. For me, the place is forever associated with great sadness. Like the night my beloved mother climbed into her bed, complaining of a horrible headache.

By the time I was fifteen, my mother was rarely well, always stressed and with a heart defect, so I thought little of it that day.

'Go to sleep, Mamma, and maybe tomorrow we'll call the doctor,' my brother Edoardo, then twenty-three, told her as he headed into his bedroom. I was left lying quite nonchalantly next to my very poorly mum. As ever, my father was absent. If only he had been there. If only we had realised how ill she was. If only we had seen the signs. These bitter regrets have haunted me since, and I know the same is true for Edoardo. I don't think either of us will ever get over the guilt of what happened next. I know I won't as long as I live.

The following morning, it was obvious from my mother's drooping mouth and her inability to speak or raise her left hand that we needed to call an ambulance to take her to hospital. Travelling with her, I held her hand and prayed hard for the best, that my worst fears would not be confirmed.

On our arrival at the hospital, Zia Mena turned up as a doctor checked over my mother. Zia Mena was always there when I needed her. I noticed that she seemed to understand what was going on and the doctor soon confirmed it: my poor, beautiful mother, aged just forty-nine, had had a stroke that took away her speech and paralysed her left side.

Although my mother recovered enough to regain her speech and most of her mobility, she never regained the use of her left arm. But almost worse than that, she relapsed mentally and seemed to revert to being a child. Who could really blame her? Nothing had gone right since we'd moved into Villa Sole. Not that we ever had a choice in the matter. Among the assets that had to be sold to pay for my father's legal fees after the police raid were Villa Simeto – our summer residence – the Moonlight club and the house opposite Villa Sole, where I had been born and brought up. My home.

Our only option, it seemed, was to move into Villa Sole, which I learned had been bequeathed to my father, alongside a large sum of money and shares in a Swiss bank, by Signor Edoardo on his death – the same year that my parents had married.

Much as I have come to appreciate Villa Sole for the beautiful house that it is – largely influenced by Richard – my initial reaction to its splendour was the same as my mother's: one of deep loathing. I hated it, totally and absolutely. Even though she never said so in as many words, I could sense that my mother did too. Back then, all I saw was an old, dark, depressing big house that wasn't my home. I cried for days, as did my mother. Utterly furious about the decision, I almost resented her for not leaving my father.

What I didn't realise then was that there was a very simple reason for not doing so: she loved him. In a very strange, contorted and dysfunctional way, I think he loved her too. They may both have liked to think that they stayed together for us, but trust me, I would rather they had separated. At least there could have been a chance for my mother to rebuild her life while still relatively young. It was certainly not my innocent idea of what love was. Of course, I didn't know at that stage just how deep the bond between them was, and in what circumstances it had started and what they shared…

Looking back, it's easy to pinpoint that time as the start of her descent into the deep depression that would eventually lead to a nervous breakdown. Although it was the first breakdown I was to witness, I am now certain it wasn't the first. Given my father's shenanigans, I suppose it shouldn't have been a surprise. Happy times were few and far between for any of us.

There were some though thanks to the arrival of a family who rented the little house next to the villa. In bygone days it had once been the servants' house. The head of the new family was Salvatore, a really good friend of my father. His wife Nina became my mother's close friend too, and would be an invaluable support for her for many difficult years to come. Giusy was their daughter and she had a son called Marco, who was by far the cutest boy I had ever seen in my young life. We all became close, and I would spend most of my days in their house rather than in my own. Through my child's eyes I sensed that it was a happy place and it represented an escape from my unhappy home.

After some time, Giusy had another child, a girl called Mara, which means 'eternally beautiful'. She really was a beautiful baby, who brought so much joy to everyone – including my mother, who affectionately called her Paperotta, meaning 'little duckling'. Happily, our relationship lasted and Mara – who I now consider my little sister – and I now have daughters the same age. She started her family so much younger than I did!

Nevertheless, there are even bad memories attached to that family friendship. One evening, when I was eleven or twelve, I was eating supper there, as I often did, when Giusy innocently asked me a question that shocked me to the core: 'Do you know where your father is tonight, Beatrice? At home with your mum? Or staying in Catania with his mistress?'

I didn't know for certain what a mistress even was, but I must have sensed it wasn't anything good or normal, dropping my food-laden fork straight onto the pretty linen tablecloth. Giusy, immediately realising from my reaction and her mother's scowl that she had dropped a bombshell, was mortified. I know she would never have said anything with ill intent and she swiftly started fussing around me apologetically.

Feeling naive and silly, as it looked as if everyone knew except me, I sat there stunned, recalling a previous conversation that I'd heard not long before between my parents: my father had told my mother in a strangely calm manner, 'You live your life, I live mine!' Both thought nobody else had heard, but my brother and I were listening to every word. I was later to discover that my brother had already known about the mistress for some time.

I assumed it meant my father would be leaving us for good, which might have actually been a relief. But no, how silly of me. It didn't mean that at all. It meant that he would continue doing exactly the same as he'd been doing for years: living Monday to Friday with his mistress in Catania, where he worked, and coming home to family life at weekends. The problem with the whole ridiculous set-up was that he did live his life, but my mother – who deserved so much better – did not.

I've never forgotten that conversation. I used to have such an idealistic image of my father. To me, he was an independent, smart, charming, clever man who could make me laugh. I once even told my cousin Marianna that I wanted to marry somebody just like him. I wonder if she knew the truth and was thinking, *Oh no, you don't want to do that!*

Where on earth did I seal away all the disappointments he'd caused over the years? All the Christmases he didn't turn up; all the ballet shows he'd missed. I only have one photograph of him holding my hand – was that not strange in itself? Looking back, I should have realised that all of my mother's tears were because of him.

There were tears aplenty from us all when my father decided to sell the house next door and our lovely friends had to move out. We were all devastated, but it was so much worse for my mother. For her, it really was the last straw, coming at a time when I was gaining a degree of independence and Edoardo was always out and about enjoying himself with his friends.

When Nina left, my mother grew ever more depressed and more scared of being lonely. Consequently she became more attached to me. Like my father, she had always been a heavy smoker – a habit Edoardo and I both hated – and there was no chance of her stopping now. Now I can understand how she must have felt. She was desperately lonely and terrified of what the future held for her.

Zia Mena once told me that my mother had desperately wanted another child after my brother, even though she knew about my father's affair by then. She wanted a girl to keep her company, as she was already predicting a solitary, sad old age. Obviously, she didn't feel she could count on Edoardo in the same way, by the mere fact that he was a boy. So, when I was born, I had a duty to fulfil from the very start. Such a big responsibility for a baby. Certainly, in those couple of years after Nina left, I felt every single bit of the weight that lay so heavily on my shoulders. Those were my teenage years, full of excitement, changes, strong emotions and hormones all over the place. But certainly not as carefree as they should have been.

My respite from the numerous problems unfolding at home came in the form of my best friend from school, Anna. From the very young age at which we met, we just clicked, even though Anna was everything I didn't feel I was: pretty, confident, determined and, most of all, utterly hilarious. Soon we were inseparable, and it was thanks to her that I became more streetwise and that my own lighter, funnier side emerged. Together we had some of the best laughs I think I've ever had, before our friendship or since.

Despite being complete opposites, we were the perfect match. Anna would dress in miniskirts and high heels, while

I was very much a casual jeans-and-trainers kind of girl. We would walk in the street and she'd have lusty boys and builders alike turning around and making comments to her. She would just laugh it off, but I'd be livid and tell them where to get off. Then we'd laugh together at their cheek. Anna was always very confident and comfortable with her femininity, whereas I was not. I always felt invisible next to her, but it never bothered me. I wasn't jealous – she had her personality and I was somehow developing mine.

Our secondary school was an all-girls' school run by nuns. During my time there, I made up my own mind about the Catholic Church and its institution. Nonetheless, we had so much fun, breaking the rules – like meeting boys at the gate at break time.

It was Anna who arranged my date with my first boyfriend Eugenio at fourteen. She was getting bored with him not plucking up the courage to ask me out, so she cheekily marched up to him and told him that if he liked me then he should ask me out! He did, and the three of us became inseparable after that. I was, however, not ready for a serious relationship, so although he was the kindest and most incredibly patient boy I could have had the good fortune to meet, it didn't last. My mother adored him much more than I ever could, and she was very cross with me when we split up after a year or so. Apparently, I didn't deserve him! Perhaps she didn't wish me to repeat her mistakes.

After sitting my exams – the equivalent of English GCSEs – my ambition was to go to the Liceo Artistico – an art school. However, I was only fourteen and my mother wasn't keen on me travelling and it was considered too far for me to commute. So I was sent off to accountancy school, a perfectly bad choice for me, given my hatred of numbers. I would rather have died than become an accountant. Unfortunately for me, in those days, my only other choice was to stay in the all-girls' secondary school for another five years and train to become a teacher, which I wanted to do even less. So it was the lesser of two evils as far as my career choice was concerned.

Fortunately, Anna was little short of a genius at maths. I hated the subject but was very good at literacy, so we helped each other out and it worked well. I accepted my destiny and spent the next five years struggling with numbers, but at least I was with my best friend! There were other subjects I liked too – Law, French and English – and I did develop other interests and make other friends, which was just as well, as Anna had a serious boyfriend by that stage. I started to have more friends and different interests, but she was always my best and truest friend. Over the years, various people, jealous of our closeness, tried to break this bond, but I'm very pleased to say that it was all without any success.

Despite my mother's growing dependence on me, I remained incredibly close to her too. Gradually our relationship, which had been so comfortable that I would sometimes sit watching TV on her lap right up to my teenage years, grew into a woman-to-woman relationship. She would ask me if a skirt was too short for her or if her hair looked better longer and I would confide in her about my relationship with my boyfriend.

It wasn't all plain sailing though, as you might expect. I can vividly remember the night of the end-of-year school ball, where everyone could attend even if you weren't leaving that year. I so desperately wanted to go, but she wouldn't let me because she wasn't feeling well. I wouldn't accept 'no' for an answer and begged her to let me go, but she resisted. I resented her so much for that.

Finally, out of sheer desperation, I called Nina and asked her to come round to keep her company. She dropped everything and did just that. I don't think my mother ever really forgave me for that, and eventually I did regret it terribly. She wasn't very well at all by then and was battling with high blood pressure, as she had done for a long time. Her worsening depression and anxiety compounded her problems, and the last thing she needed was a stroppy teenage daughter.

It wasn't too long after that that she had the stroke. There wasn't much laughter in that house after that. To say that the following three years were horrendous is an understatement. I could never have predicted how my life would be turned upside down in just one night.

The day after, when I went to see her in hospital and looked into her vacant eyes, it should have been obvious to me that my beautiful mum was gone forever. In that moment, I didn't fully understand how serious it was or realise that this was a permanent condition, but it didn't take long before I did. The one person who'd had the capacity, no matter what happened to me, to make me feel loved, secure and protected was gone. The mother that was left was somebody who depended on me. It was a complete role reversal and not one I was remotely prepared for. I still needed her; I so very desperately needed her.

Those first few weeks and months are now just a sad blur. Luckily, my wonderful Zia Mena once again stepped in to take charge for a while. She would come to the house and look after us all, and we eventually got into a routine of sorts. She would arrive before school time and my brother and I would help get Mum ready for the day ahead – get her up, wash her, feed her. After breakfast I would wait for Anna, who was always behind schedule, then go to school. We would use the excuse of my mother's illness for being late, but really it was all Anna's fault.

After school, Zia Mena would have lunch ready, then in the early afternoon she would return home, leaving Edoardo and I in charge of care again. We would take turns for the night shift, which meant getting up several times as Mum often needed the toilet. Because of her paralysis, she wasn't able to eat, drink or be self-sufficient in any way. For a while, she had physiotherapy and slowly started to walk again. She couldn't walk without dragging her leg, but at least she was no longer in a wheelchair. Unfortunately, she never regained the use of her arm, so remained dependent on us.

At first, we naively thought it would be a temporary arrangement, but several months down the line it became abundantly clear that our mother's situation would not improve. This was it now – her life and ours.

With Zia Mena's help, we struggled on, still numb and confused but with some sort of security that she was there to support us in the demanding roles that had been forced upon us. My brother was at university studying economics and he absorbed himself in his studies. He was very disciplined and tried to juggle academic work with looking after our mother as much as he could.

Everything took a turn for the worse the day Zia Mena had a nervous breakdown herself and was unable to come and help out anymore. Both my cousins lived abroad, and Zio Ruggero was still working on a cruise ship. So I ended up going to school in the morning, looking after my mother during the day and then spending the night at Zia Mena's to help and look after her.

It wasn't long before Zio Ruggero retired and I learned that after a horrendous argument with my father, he had forbidden our kind and wonderful aunt to come to our house again. Well done, Father! As if we hadn't suffered enough already, you decided to deprive us of the only person who could help, support and alleviate our pain. In her place, he employed a local woman who would come and spend time with my mother while I was at school. Any spare time I had was used to look after Mum and improvise as a housekeeper.

Somehow, purely because I was a girl, my father expected me to know how to be the perfect housewife. It clearly didn't register that it might be a problem for me. After all, I was only fifteen, and up until that point I had always had a devoted mother to do everything for me. He was my father, and although he had never behaved as such, he improvised also and failed miserably. All of a sudden, he tried to be an authoritative parent, always trying to discipline me. In truth, he was so bad at it, it was almost comical. Where had his parenting been when we needed it – when we would have appreciated a bit of support to go out at weekends like other normal young people? Instead, we were made to feel guilty for wanting a break.

I will never forget one late summer afternoon when I had managed to get out for a few hours. I came back into the house and through the dining-room window I could see mother and father sitting in the courtyard, talking under the mandarin tree. My mother looked so sad, sitting there with her head down, tilted to one side, shoulders slumped like a person who had lost all will to go on. Momentarily, my eyes moved to the wall next to the window where there hung a black-and-white photograph of Mum. She must have been about eighteen and was so beautiful, with her radiant, infectious smile. She looked like a movie star with her fifties' hairstyle, white off-the-shoulder top and a triple strand of pearls around her neck. So very different from the woman before me then.

From time to time, I noticed she was looking at him as if to say, *I really don't want to listen to this but I can't just get up and go. Please stop.* Then I heard what he was saying to her. 'You see? They don't love you! As soon as I arrive, they can't wait to go and leave you. Can't you see you're a burden to them?'

I don't think I had ever hated him more than in that moment. Hate isn't a strong enough word. I felt sick with disgust to think that anyone could do anything like this. All my mother had left in her life was my brother and me, and she had already suffered tremendously knowing how much her illness affected us. He wanted to take away every little piece of happiness she felt. Why? To get back at us? To make her need him more?

I walked out into the courtyard, looking straight at him, and he knew how I was feeling – full of hate and disgust. Why could he not be the frail, vulnerable one sitting in that chair, so easy to hurt and destroy?

'Come on, Mum,' I said, offering her my arm to help her get up. 'Let's go for a walk around the garden. It's time for your afternoon exercise.'

From that day on, after hearing my father say those terrible things, my attitude changed completely. It was a turning point in our relationship, and I became more assertive, argumentative and confrontational towards him. Obviously, the whole situation at home was affecting me deeply though. I had exams to get through, and it took me a good while to find my way. In those days, I didn't understand how Edoardo could keep going as if nothing out of the ordinary was happening. Now I know and understand that his own way of coping was to concentrate on his studies. It was his escape.

From that point on, my mother had the haunted stare of a lost child crying out for help. The feeling of not having been able to help her, or the fearful child who lived inside her, was unbearable. But somehow, I learned to live with it, even though it never stopped hurting. It still hurts now when I think about it.

There is a particular episode that haunts me even now: the afternoon that she went to the bathroom by herself and never came back. I was watching TV with Edoardo and completely immersed in my own teenage thoughts, an indulgence I didn't often have the luxury of.

Suddenly I realised that she'd been gone for what seemed ages, though in reality it was probably only about twenty minutes. Jumping off the sofa, I instinctively ran towards the bathroom. My head was filled with all sorts of fearful imaginings, but then I saw her. She was standing completely still with tears streaming down her face, quietly resigned to her sad life. The problem? She couldn't walk up the step. The one small step that divided the library from the dining room before the kitchen-cum-lounge where we were sitting.

She whispered humbly, 'I didn't want to disturb you…' The look in her eyes is something I will never be able to forget, and unfortunately it replaced her old smiling face in my memory for a long, long time afterwards.

That was the day I found myself wishing with all my heart that my own beautiful mother would die peacefully to escape this living hell she was enduring. I felt incredibly guilty and ashamed, but I couldn't help the way I felt. To me she was already dead. She had died the day she'd had the stroke. There was nothing left of her feisty old self. It had taken everything from her, certainly every last scrap of her dignity.

Having to rely on your children to feed you and wash your naked, devastated body can't have been easy for her either. Especially when one of the children carrying out these intimate care duties was her son, who was by then a young man. Could there be anything worse for a mother? No, according to my mother's face. It was a mix of shame, shyness, helplessness and apology. And I just knew that somewhere in her mind she was thinking, *This is not how I want my children to remember me.*

It's because of that *look* that I made up my young mind about a very important matter of life and death. *If I ever have children,* I vowed to myself, *I will never allow them to see me like this. Euthanasia has to be the answer.* Nothing since has changed my mind and I stand by that decision today, now that I am indeed a mother myself. My husband Richard knows and fully understands my wishes. The biggest gift I could ever offer my own offspring would be to ensure that they remember me as their mum – their real mum. Not a frail, dependent shadow of my former self. My mother had become a ghost, nothing more.

9

A True Blessing

Padre Giovanni
(Priest of Santa Caterina Church, Taormina, May 1947)

A s I relax in the shade of the mandarin tree at Villa Sole, enjoying my weekly chat with Signor Edward Cecil Page over a cup of Earl Grey tea and a few dainty sandwiches and biscuits, I can't help but wonder what I ever did on Wednesday afternoons before this. Our meetings have become a little ritual that I look forward to all week long. My secret pleasure.

The Baron is such a genuinely kind, educated, interesting gentleman, and our discussions satiate my intellectual hunger in a way I didn't imagine possible after leaving Rome for this poor town. To think I had such doubts about striking up a conversation in the first place! I must tell him about that one day. It would surely give us both a chuckle, but I'll wait for a moment when a little light-heartedness is called for, like when one of our discussions becomes heated, as they sometimes do. Whatever that old proverb might say, great minds do not always think alike! Ha!

I'd just finished my Sunday evening Mass and was standing outside Santa Caterina, bidding goodbye to my parishioners, when Signor Edoardo passed by with a local gentleman that I now know as his loyal right-hand man, Rosario Privitera. This is the man who is responsible for the smooth running of his magnificent estate.

Ever since I arrived a few months ago, I'd been wondering about approaching the Baron, as I'd heard so much about his good work around here, helping these poor families by providing employment for their youngsters. But – and I'm quite ashamed to admit this – I'd hesitated because I knew he belonged to a different church – the Church of England. I didn't know what his attitude would be towards a Catholic priest. Maybe even one of disdain... and as I don't speak English, how would we even converse? That night, though, I found the courage to speak to him; perhaps I was fortified by the day's Masses going so well. *After all, we believe in the same God, so why not?* I reasoned.

'*Buongiorno... Vostra Eccellenza* – Good day... Your Excellency,' I addressed him with a slight hesitancy. Was that the correct way to address him? I had never crossed paths with an English gentleman before, so how was I to know?

I needn't have worried though. With a smile of amused embarrassment, he stopped dead in his tracks and corrected me. 'No, no! Not *Vostra Eccellenza*. Please! Call me Signor Edoardo like everyone else.'

Turning to instruct his companion Privitera to carry on ahead, he then came closer and struck up a pleasant conversation with me in perfect Italian, spoken with a soft, charming English accent. I have since discovered that his grasp of the Sicilian language is pretty impressive too.

Noticing that the local children were hanging around me excitedly, hoping for their Sunday treats of *caramelle alla carruba* (dark, sticky sweets made from the fruit of the carob tree, a sort of poor man's chocolate), Signor Edoardo asked what they were doing. I explained that it was a tradition that my predecessor had started and suggested I continue. I had done so, and realising that it was such a highlight for them, I was happy to carry on.

'Don't let me stop you,' he urged, so I emptied my pockets and they ran off, chewing noisily but happily, leaving us free to chat uninterrupted.

Signor Edoardo looked quite moved that such a simple gesture had elicited so much pleasure, and after exchanging a few pleasantries he invited me to have afternoon tea with him at Villa Sole the following day to discuss a project he had in mind. Intrigued, I accepted graciously, hopeful of learning more about his beliefs.

As it transpired, the meeting was to discuss the possibility of him funding the building and running costs of a church youth centre for the same urchins of Taormina begging me for *caramelle alla carruba* every week. It was something he'd been thinking about for some time! So everything I'd heard about this man's generosity really was sincere.

Signor Edoardo was true to his word all right. Working together to set his wonderful altruistic plan in motion, we finally achieved our goal just yesterday. And what a day it was to wait for!

The doors of the brand-new Centro Salesiani Don Bosco, rapidly built using local labour, officially opened at 2 p.m. Instead of dicing with their lives by playing hide-and-seek in the still-uncleared dangerous remains of houses destroyed by enemy bombers during the war, the local children were able to gather in safety to indulge in their games, football or whatever, and just be kids. God willing, that will be Signor Edoardo's legacy for generations of children to come. In Taormina, he will always be remembered and revered for his sublime generosity. He is a true blessing for this community. And I for one am honoured and humbled to now call him a good friend. Long may our friendship continue.

10

Be Careful What You Wish For

To this very day, if there is one piece of music that brings tears to my eyes whenever I hear it, it's the soundtrack to 1978 film *The Deer Hunter*. I am probably not alone. It's a haunting piece, but for me, the reaction it provokes is a purely personal one.

It was a wet, dark evening in December and there wasn't a soul in the streets. The place was like a ghost town. It wasn't until I moved to England that I realised that outside of Sicily, the entire world doesn't stop just because it's raining. My brother Edoardo and I were at his friend Luca's house watching a movie. As I grew, the age gap between us seemed progressively less and we started to have more friends in common. Occasionally, we even went out together.

Luca has been a friend of the family for years. His father, a doctor, brought both myself and my brother into the world, and Luca's brother was a GP – our family's GP, no less. Just like them, Luca was planning a career in medicine, which he has since achieved – he is now a successful gynaecologist.

I love Robert De Niro and was enjoying the film until the telephone interrupted our viewing halfway through and we had to pause it. Luca went to answer it and told us that his brother Paolo had called.

'Your dad rang and says your mum isn't well. You should go. Now!' he announced.

Although we didn't have any more information than that, his tone was one of urgency – no doubt passed down the line from our father. Instinctively we knew it wasn't going to be good news, that it was going to be something serious. Another stroke maybe – with more devastating consequences this time? Our hearts sank at the prospect.

Edoardo and I raced home as if our own lives depended on it, and within ten minutes of receiving the call, we were running towards Villa Sole and into our mother's bedroom. As soon as I stepped through the door and saw her lying on the bed, I knew that it was serious all right. I thought: *There's something not right about the way she's lying down… it's unnatural.* Maybe it was the way her head was turned to one side, or the way her left arm was hanging limply over the bed, or that her lips were slightly open…

We went straight to her bedside, where we sat and softly whispered her name. Her beautiful green-flecked brown eyes were open very slightly, but as soon as she heard our voices, they closed and a solitary tear ran down her face.

Then, suddenly, she was no longer with us. She was gone. It was obvious to us both that our mother had been waiting for us, waiting for us to arrive before finally leaving us and this life that had become nothing more than a sad existence for the past three years. A painful, drawn-out death.

As we walked out of the bedroom, Edoardo said, 'She's not suffering anymore. Wherever she is, it has to be a better place than this…'

They were my own thoughts entirely, but the difference was that I couldn't find my voice like he could. I couldn't bring myself to actually say the words that were running round my head. It's very possible that even at that early stage, I was deeply ashamed of the sense of relief I was feeling. Only Edoardo and my father could understand that. Although I'm not so sure that my father's understanding was for the same reasons.

Not long afterwards, I realised that my mother's 'unnatural' position was due to my father trying to move her after she'd had a heart attack. What he was hoping to achieve, I don't know. Resuscitate her? Tell her something important? Like he was sorry for causing her so much sorrow for so long? Living his own life but not allowing her to live hers?

It must have been around 11 p.m. when the house began to fill up with people – a mix of friends, neighbours and family. Everyone, it seemed, except anyone who really mattered to us. Even Zia Mena was missing. She and Zio Ruggero were with their son Mattia in Turin, where they normally spent a few months every winter. Sometimes longer.

All around us, people were saying how sorry they were for our loss. And all I could think, bitterly, was, *Our loss?* It hadn't just happened now. I had lost my mother, my friend, the one person I loved so unconditionally, three years ago. Yet nobody told me they felt sorry for my loss then! Where were all these people when my mother was alive? When she was struggling on a daily basis just to put one foot in front of the other? When she could have really done with their sympathy and a bit of practical help?

Angry and upset, I knew I had to get out of there. My brother just disappeared off to his bedroom to grieve alone, and he didn't come out again until the following morning. Knowing Edoardo as I do, if anyone had attempted to talk to him in that state, they would have regretted it.

Soon Anna and her mother, Signora Caterina, arrived and they must have instinctively realised how I was feeling because they took me back to the relative calm of their own home. I don't know whose idea it was, but it was a good one. I spent a lot of time there, and it felt natural to be there. Anna had a sister and two brothers so it was a busy house, yet it was never a problem to set another place at the table or host a last-minute sleepover. I had always felt part of this family, and that night I was so relieved to escape the crowd in my house.

Anna and I slept in her mother and father's big bed that night. It wasn't something we had ever done before. But I vividly remember us lying there quietly in the dark. Then Anna must have said something funny and we both started laughing. Hysterically. It was the kind of laughter that goes on forever. Every time we calmed down and looked at each other, we would start again! Like those carefree times when we were driving round and round the streets of Taormina for hours on end in Anna's Fiat 500 without actually going anywhere. I laughed so much, lying there in her parents' bed.

Then I suddenly stopped and began sobbing. Until that moment I hadn't shed a single tear, but I made up for it when I started. The floodgates opened and I wept and wept, unable to stop for a second. It went on for so long that my relentless bawling made my jaws hurt and I could barely open my mouth. When I did, I found myself confiding in Anna about the deep shame I was feeling for being so relieved that my poor mother had died.

I will never forget how very matter-of-fact she was or her kindness as she listened patiently to my confession. She reassured me that I wasn't a monster for thinking that way, that I was just a daughter who loved her mother very much, that it was a perfectly understandable reaction in such sad and extreme circumstances. I will always be grateful to my dear, dear friend for those words of reassurance.

The following morning, I went back home and Anna insisted on accompanying me. When we got there, I was stunned to find that all those people who had suddenly descended on us, so rudely intruding on our raw grief the previous night, were still there, busily running around arranging things.

The minute I walked through the door, one of the unfamiliar women rushed straight up to me and asked me to get some clothes for my mother to wear in her coffin. Taken aback by that complete lack of sensitivity towards me, a distraught eighteen-year-old girl who had just lost her mother, I snapped back angrily. Whoever that stranger was – probably one of our aunts who'd been invisible to us up until that point – she must have immediately regretted her words.

Choosing clothes! That would have meant having to go into my mother's bedroom while she was still lying there, completely lifeless. I didn't want to see her like that or remember her like that. Why on earth did they think I would? Why did they think that I cared, or that she would care, about what she was wearing in her damned coffin? She hadn't cared about what she'd worn for the last three years. All sartorial pride had disappeared out of the window when she had the stroke.

Fuming, I stormed into my room with Anna. I heard some of the crowd commenting on how rude I was, but it fell on deaf ears. I wasn't going to feel guilty about my completely understandable reaction to these vultures preying on our tragic misfortune.

Protective as ever, Anna adopted the role of my bodyguard and would only allow in my true friends, who had come to visit because they genuinely cared for me, my brother and my mum. One of these was Rocco, who just hugged me.

We didn't need words. Throughout my mother's illness, he had always been on hand to help me get through the endless problems. Being my brother's best friend since a very young age, he'd been part of my life for as long as I could remember. He was one of the few friends who stuck around even after the decline of our family fortune. He and I had become very close during these last two years and had started dating. When everything was crumbling all around me, when nothing seemed real anymore, the only genuine feeling I had was towards him. When I wasn't fitting anywhere else, I fitted into his arms. My first love.

In Sicily, for some people, emotional occasions like these are seen as social opportunities to meet up and gossip. It's a chance to be indiscreet, judgemental and, most of all, act as if they actually cared. It has nothing to do with paying respect to the deceased – somebody's loved one.

I always despised all this. Pure hypocrisy. I accept that somebody has to deal with the things that need dealing with when somebody dies, and that was never going to be me or my brother. But there are ways and means of doing things. As for my father, I can't remember seeing him much at all. At the height of our grief, neither Edoardo nor I had any idea where he was or what he was doing – conspicuous by his absence, as ever.

The funeral was organised very quickly for the day afterwards. In Italy, like many other Mediterranean countries, funerals take place immediately after a person's death. As far as I was concerned, the speed was actually a good thing. The sooner it happened, the better. I really don't think I could have coped with the farce of all those strangers at home for any length of time. *Let's get it over and done with quickly* was my attitude. I even thought about not going to the funeral. Zia Mena wasn't going to be there – she was so broken by the news that she couldn't travel back from Turin. If I'm honest, I was relieved she couldn't come. Seeing her would have made everything so much more emotional for me.

Although I didn't care much about what all those people would think or say if I didn't attend my own mother's funeral, I knew I didn't want to let them jump to the conclusion that I disrespected my mother in any way. It was too hard to accept. And what about Edoardo? I had to go with him. We needed to support each other at this terrible time.

Nevertheless, I felt I had to make a stand of some sort so I purposely didn't wear black mourning clothes. When some interfering busybody or other said that I should have done, I didn't mince my words in reply.

'Mind your own business!' I told them sharply, before turning away and ignoring them. My real, vibrant mum had always loved colours. The brighter and more vivid, the better. So why would I wear a drab outfit that she'd have hated to say my official goodbyes?

All the way to the cathedral, Edoardo and I held hands, and did so again on our way from the church to the cemetery. I can't remember us ever holding hands before in our lives, but it just felt like the right thing to do, to cling to each other. We didn't say very much – we just did what we had to do as respectable children burying their mother.

In church we even stood alongside our father, painfully shaking the hands of endless people queuing up to pay their condolences. Hundreds of hands. Most of the hands and the serious faces attached to them meant absolutely nothing to me. But every now and again, somebody that really mattered to me, or mattered to my mother, would appear, and their genuine pain ignited my own. Out of nowhere the tears gushed in another endless stream. The whole experience was mentally and physically exhausting.

Rocco was there, which was comforting to both Edoardo and me. Once more, Anna, who hadn't left my side for the last forty-eight hours, was on hand to rescue me in my darkest hour by dragging me away from that sad scene that has been etched on my mind ever since. *Grazie*, Anna. Thank you so much.

11

The Son He Never Had

Padre Giovanni
(Priest of Santa Caterina Church, Taormina, October 1947)

Once more I am passing another very pleasant Wednesday afternoon at Villa Sole, and yet again I am witnessing the extraordinary kindness of my good friend Signor Edoardo, the big-hearted baron from England. Several months have passed since we first started this little routine, and even though I know him so much better now, he still manages to surprise me with his overwhelming largesse.

The Centro Salesiani Don Bosco project was completed quickly after its conception and has already been a roaring success for the poor young people of this town, thanks not just to Signor Edoardo's enduring financial support but also to his keen personal interest. Often on his regular strolls around town he will take the time to pop in and observe how the young generation enjoy their games. Sometimes he will single out one or two of the boys and engage them in an animated conversation about their lives. He always shows such a keen interest in what they enjoy doing, quizzing them about what makes them excited and happy.

I've always thought that with his naturally kind, fatherly manner, it's such a shame that he never joined the priesthood himself or found a wife to enjoy an intimate family life of his own. I have no doubts that he would make a wonderful father of either variety. But from what he's just told me, he's just secured the next best thing by unofficially 'adopting' young Ciccio, that cheeky but handsome houseboy who was fortunate enough to get a job here a year ago.

Maybe when he's visiting the Centro Salesiani Don Bosco he's eyeing up his next willing apprentice for the estate, I don't know. After all, it can't be easy keeping this place ticking over as efficiently as it seems to do. Almost like clockwork. It must take the enduring hard work, effort and commitment of loyal and dedicated staff to deliver the luxurious level of hospitality he offers so often. There are always guests coming and going, and they are unfailingly treated to nothing but the best food, drink and entertainment.

Occasionally, they venture out of the estate during their stay and will be seen in the bars, restaurants and shops of the town. Handsome, dapper men and beautiful, expensively dressed women from all over the continent and beyond, eager to travel here any time to enjoy the Baron's renowned lavish entertainment and his legendary bonhomie. They stand out like sore thumbs in all their finery amid the poverty around here.

I always thought that Privitera took on the lion's share of the organisation and maintenance that makes Villa Sole so enticing to these glamorous guests, but a few whispers I've heard in the town suggest his gambling foibles are getting the better of him and the biggest part of his day seems to be spent playing cards. But as a servant of God, it's certainly not my place to take heed of idle gossip. After all, who are we to judge? Only God has that right.

With the biggest heart and best will in the world, Signor Edoardo cannot relieve the burden of our town's despairing mothers by taking in all their children to provide them with a better life, the way he's done with Ciccio. Although I'm sure he would if he could.

Today, as I bask in the garden with this great man, sipping a cold glass of his favourite English beer, Bass, I marvel at the way his face suddenly lights up when Ciccio appears, prompting him to tell me about the 'adoption', which is his promise to look after him as a parent would, ensuring him a degree of financial security for life. It's abundantly clear that he treats him like the son he never had. And I'm happy for him that his benevolence carries its own rewards. Love comes in so many forms.

12
The Great Grief Escape

The resentment I felt towards my father only escalated after the funeral, so when, completely out of the blue, I was asked if I fancied escaping to Australia with friends, it took me just minutes to make up my mind.

'Yes please!' I answered, leaping at the chance to start a new life on the other side of the world with lovely people that I liked and trusted. Why would I not?

The months after burying our mother had been tough. Neither Edoardo nor I could have envisaged what might happen next, and we lived our lives from one day to the next as we tried to get used to our new freedom. It was strange no longer having Mum to care for, as the past three years had largely revolved around her and her needs. As much as it had been a struggle for us, those demands had also given a structure to our days and suddenly we missed that in a strange kind of way.

My relationship with my father had unsurprisingly been tense. He still didn't know how to be a father, because he had never been one. He'd always left the education and discipline to my mother, and then when her health failed, he'd left most of her care to us. He was continuing to act like a very poor imitation of an involved parent and, quite honestly, I would have respected him more if he hadn't tried. It was a case of far too little, far too late.

I continued to be confrontational and argumentative, which only stoked things up, of course. Interestingly, he didn't try this behaviour with Edoardo. My brother had always had a friendlier relationship with him.

That's not to say they didn't still have arguments though. During one particular disagreement, I think my father was actually afraid of his physically stronger son. So he reserved all his late-life parenting skills for me. What luck!

It was during one of these new 'paternal' phases that he decided to teach me a lesson and lock me out of the house because I was late home after an evening out at a local pizzeria with friends. On arriving back twenty minutes after my 10 p.m. curfew, I found all three entrances to Villa Sole locked. So I was considered old enough and responsible enough to look after my invalid mother and run the house while studying for my GCSEs, but I wasn't allowed to be twenty minutes late? Interesting logic!

With no mobile phones back then, all I could do was stand shivering in the chilly, dark garden and bang on the door nearest Edoardo's bedroom until he realised what was going on and let me in.

Suddenly, out of nowhere, my father appeared and began yelling at me. 'You are a disgrace of a daughter!' he ranted.

Furious, I shouted right back at him at the top of my voice. 'No, you are the disgrace! Call yourself a father?'

His response was short and to the point. 'Slut!'

How dare he? Now completely beside myself with rage, I found myself spewing out everything I'd wanted to say for years. All the anger and disgust I harboured towards him just poured out of me like hot lava. Loudly, slowly and clearly; controlled bile. I didn't want him to miss anything I had to say. I surprised myself with my boldness. It was just like the scene I had rehearsed in my head so many times. I had even dreamed about it.

Things went on like that for some time afterwards, until my father made a sudden announcement, not even three months after my mother's funeral. I was sitting reading under the mandarin tree in the garden one afternoon when he told me, quite matter-of-factly: 'I'm getting married and Petronilla is coming to live here.'

To be fair, he never said or even intimated that Edoardo and I had to go, but we both knew that we couldn't live under the same roof as the pair of them and that we needed to leave Villa Sole sooner rather than later. Although my father said we could stay, I doubt he meant it. He knew perfectly well that we would rather live in a cave than with him and his new wife; he was on a safe bet with that invitation. And when builders arrived in my bedroom at six thirty one morning to begin renovation work in preparation for her moving in, it was a signal that it was time to move on.

Edoardo and I packed up our belongings and rented a dingy one-bedroomed flat in town that was only a step up from a cave. In fact, that's exactly what we called it – 'The Cave'!

In Villa Sole, we had each had spacious bedrooms at opposite ends of the house. Here, in this gloomy hovel, we had the ignominy of sharing a cramped bedroom. The living room had no windows, and the bathroom and kitchen were tiny. No fresh oranges to pick from my balcony in the mornings here.

Although my father promised to help with the rent, he rarely did. Miraculously, I had passed all my exams. So, after a discussion with Zia Mena and Edoardo, we all agreed that I would work to support us both until my brother finished his studies, and Zia Mena would help out financially here and there. She was there for us once again.

After Edoardo had received his degree, I finally did enrol to study law. But I wasn't destined to follow my academic dreams. After a year of study and taking a few exams, I had to pause my studies as Edoardo was taking time to get established in his career, which meant that he wasn't earning enough to support me. So, we agreed once again that I would take a break from studying and get a job to help support the both of us. I didn't know it then, but the months turned into years, and eventually I realised that my studies had stopped for good rather than simply being put on hold. The dreams of the career I would have faded, life having chosen a different path for me.

Before my mother's death, I'd worked a few summer shifts at a takeaway restaurant in town, which was quite a novelty in Sicily in the eighties. Italians all love their food and it has to be good, so high standards were necessary. I have to say the dishes were cooked from scratch daily and were absolutely delicious. The business was owned by a married couple, Ottavia and Saverio, who were originally from Lipari, an island north of Sicily. After emigrating to Australia a decade previously, they had decided to return with their young family. Thankfully, the restaurant was doing well and they were happy to employ me.

By now, my relationship with Rocco was coming to an end. Maybe the age difference was the main reason, or perhaps it simply wasn't meant to be. What I do know is that the love and support he gave me was the reason I managed to get through the worst times without completely losing myself. We both agreed that our friendship was the most important thing.

After spending some time alone, and not looking for anything serious, I met Leonardo, who at first seemed an unlikely choice of boyfriend. Definitely not my type, he was a year younger then me and had blond hair thanks to his German mother's genes. Although I wasn't in a very stable place emotionally, given all that had happened, he didn't seem to mind and we gave our relationship a go. Why not? He loved life and lived it to the full. He was fun to be with and his positivity was infectious. In truth, he was a breath of fresh air. We hadn't been together very long – only a few months – when Ottavia and Saverio decided to return to Australia and asked if I'd like to go with them.

Poor Leonardo didn't get a second thought, even though we'd become very close in the short time we'd been together. My mind was made up though. It was time for me to spread my wings.

To be honest, when Ottavia and Saverio asked if they could talk to me, I was expecting them to say that they were closing down their business to return to Australia and my employment was being terminated. But no, they wanted me to join them, to help look after their three lovely daughters and work with them in their next venture. They also told me that I could return to Sicily any time I wanted and even offered to buy me an open-return ticket. It was an incredibly generous and kind thing to do.

Having never travelled any further than Paris, I had always had a desire to see more of the world, so it seemed like the perfect excuse to escape my grief and this heavily troubled life that I was leading. My only worry was leaving my brother, but then I decided that I could send him money from Australia, and Zia Mena was there to help anyway.

So there was me, bereft at eighteen years of age, heading Down Under for the adventure of a lifetime with the princely sum of 50,000 lira in my pocket. It may sound a lot, but back then it was roughly the equivalent of £22. For the first time I thought, *My mother is really looking after me, making sure that my path has crossed with such incredible people.* It's something I've found myself saying many more times since in my life.

Big was my first impression of Australia when we flew into that vast country. Everything seemed huge compared with Sicily: houses, roads and distances. If someone said they were 'going round the corner' for something, it could mean a two-hour car journey. Coming from a small town like Taormina, where that same phrase meant a five-minute walk, it was quite something. But it was the huge distance between myself and home that proved the most difficult thing for me to acclimatise to.

Initially it was great – a holiday really. We all lived on the outskirts of Sydney in the Italian suburb of Five Dock in the state of New South Wales, which is ten kilometres west of the city's central business district. To my delight, it was just like being in an Italian village, filled with delis, cafes and butchers. I even learned a bit of history.

Apparently, Italians had been living in Australia since before the First Fleet – eleven ships that left England in 1787 to found New South Wales. Two sailors of Italian descent, James Matra and Antonio Ponto, were aboard HMS *Endeavour* with Captain James Cook on his voyage of discovery in 1770. Subsequently, a convict called Giuseppe Tuzo arrived with the First Fleet and eventually settled in Sydney. The number of Italy-born Victorians peaked at 121,000 in 1971. Italian immigration then declined, but Italians are still the fifth-largest immigrant community in Victoria, after the English community. So, home from home? Sadly not, it turned out.

Mainly, my role was helping to look after Ottavia and Saverio's children, and from time to time I had jobs. As daunting as it was to go out and work in such unfamiliar surroundings, I pushed myself out of my comfort zone, and for a little while I worked in a fish restaurant in the popular tourist area of Manly. I helped in the kitchen, mostly doing the washing-up, cleaning and food preparation, which sometimes meant peeling hundreds of little frozen prawns. After peeling the first few kilos, I couldn't feel my fingers anymore. They were as frozen as the prawns, and, like the prawns, my skin would start to peel. Needless to say, this job didn't last long.

Sometimes I would help Saverio make garlic butter – something that I'd never seen in my life before. Contrary to popular belief, it doesn't actually originate from Italy. On the other hand, bruschetta – which has chopped tomatoes, garlic, olive oil and oregano – does. In his garden, Saverio had what I can only describe as a huge electric mixer the size of a children's paddling pool. We would put in an enormous amount of butter and mix it with garlic powder. As a consequence, the powder would get into your pores, and not even soaking in a bath for hours would get rid of the garlic smell. Not my perfume of choice.

Gradually, the novelty began to wear off and I started to feel incredibly homesick. I missed my family and friends. I hadn't really had time to properly grieve for my mother either and found it difficult being so far away from everything I knew. I also had Leonardo calling me constantly to tell me that he missed me and that if I wanted to return home, he would find me a job.

He wasn't the only one calling saying he missed me though; Rocco was doing the same thing. As sad as I was to leave this amazing family who had so magnanimously welcomed me into their home and treated me like their own relative, after six months I decided to return to Sicily and start another new chapter of my young but already eventful life. Maybe if I'd been older and more balanced emotionally, it would have been a different story, as I'd grown very fond of Ottavia, who was like the big sister I never had. Later, I would miss her a great deal.

On arriving at Catania Airport, sticky and exhausted from the long flight, the first thing I saw was a huge bunch of red roses being held by a tanned blond man who looked like a windsurfer. Leonardo! There was no doubt, he knew how to make a girl feel special. True to his word, Leonardo had also secured me a job as an assistant in a jewellery shop in the main street, Corso Umberto, in Taormina.

For about two years we enjoyed a carefree and easy relationship, spending our weekends together on the beach in summer so Leonardo could windsurf. Then in winter, we would spend weekends in the Mount Etna region, where he had a snowboarding school, and also we would spend *la settimana bianca* – the white week – in prestigious ski resorts in the Italian Alps. It could have been perfect, except that I underestimated the bond I'd created with Rocco during the hardest point of my life.

In the end, I was honest with myself and Leonardo, and we agreed to break up. Although not proud of my behaviour, I excused it by saying I was too messed up by the trauma of the last few years. I wasn't an easy person to save, but Leonardo tried endlessly as I battled to escape the misery of my difficult past. It wasn't letting me escape though, and slowly but steadily I was going downhill.

There was nothing that I or anyone else could do about it. So it was better for me to be alone and not hurting anyone else.

13
Crushed

Linetta Greco
(Twelve-year-old daughter of head cook at Villa Sole. June 1948)

Even from the far corner of the big garden at Villa Sole, I can hear Mamma's voice shouting me: 'Linetta! Linetta! Where are you? Come quickly. *Sbrigati*! – Hurry up!'

Scooping up the posy of deep magenta bougainvillea that I've been picking, I jump to attention and, with my friend Ciccio racing alongside me, head down the dusty path to the kitchen door, where she's waiting for me.

'Ah, good girl, you've done it. Now go and put them in a vase full of water, take it up to Signor Edoardo's room and place it carefully on top of his dresser,' she orders.

Today, Signor Edoardo is returning from one of his exotic trips. By now, he'll be on his way back in the same motorcar he takes Ciccio and I out for rides in, and while he's telling his driver to hurry along the sea road, I bet he's dreaming of a nice cup of tea under his beloved mandarin tree in the courtyard.

It's a warm, humid day – not the scorching heat you would feel in August, but still hot enough to make your skin feel sticky and uncomfortable. Signor Edoardo always complains how the thick dust in the air, lifted by the car wheels on the sun-baked old road, makes him cough. He constantly moans to Mamma about how he finds the heat oppressive at this time of year and how he longs for rain, even though he knows it won't come. Well, not the sort of rain that would come in the middle of a steamy English summer. Here, the sky barely dampens even when we finally get a downpour. I can't even imagine a place where it rains heavily and continuously in summer!

Dutifully, I place the flowers as Mamma told me and quickly run back downstairs in time to hear the screech of the brakes of Signor's car in the pebbled drive.

'*E' arrivato*! – He's here!' I yell to Mamma, who's disappeared into the dining room.

She's been preparing for his arrival for days, and I don't want her to miss it any more than I want to miss it myself. Whenever he comes back from one of his long foreign trips, there's always great excitement to see what he's brought back with him. Who knows what present he'll bring me this time? Another doll perhaps! Or colouring pencils? Mamma likes to see the strange food he brings from the places we can only dream of going.

'Why doesn't he ever take you with him, Ciccio?' I ask but he just shrugs.

'One day perhaps?' I smile at him and he nods: 'Maybe.'

If he were my father, I wouldn't stop begging to go with him so I could get a glimpse of the outside world and all its treasures. Villa Sole is full of its strange objects, beautiful paintings and artefacts from mysterious lands. It's fascinating, magical even.

I follow Ciccio into the courtyard to greet Signor Edoardo. But while Ciccio runs up and hugs him, I hold back as he returns the embrace. He looks so happy to be home again. Mamma ushers me back inside behind them. In the hallway, Signor Edoardo reaches down into his brown leather travel bag and pulls out a brightly-coloured paper parcel.

'Have you been a good boy while I've been away?' he asks Ciccio, who nods furiously. 'OK, then, here you are,' he says with a chuckle as he hands it over.

I watch curiously as Ciccio rips off the paper and finds two ceramic drums – one big, one small.

'It's called a Tam Tam bongo and it's from Morocco,' he tells him as Ciccio tries to play it.

Signor Edoardo laughs loudly, then turns to me. 'I have a present for you too, pretty little Linetta, and one for your sister Mena, but you'll both have to wait until I've had a bath, as they're in another suitcase and I need to wash away the dust that has got into every pore of my body.'

I smile, pretending not to mind, and try to look grateful, but I can't help feeling jealous of Ciccio. His drums are lovely, with brightly coloured geometrical patterns decorating their bases. Why do I have to wait for my present when he doesn't? And why do I always have to be second best? If it's not to Ciccio, it's to Mena.

Putting on a brave face, I notice the pile of unopened post on the hall table next to another vase of bougainvillea I'd picked earlier in the day. Keen to get into his good books and hurry him into checking his cases, I pick up the important-looking thick parchment envelopes to give to Signor Edoardo.

'*La posta* – the mail,' I say cheerily, but he ignores me completely and is already disappearing up the stairs to his bathroom, where I can hear somebody running a cool bath for him.

I give up trying to impress him and instead ask Ciccio to come back out into the garden with me, where I hope he'll allow me to have a turn on his new drums.

Just as he agrees, Signor Edoardo stops still and turns round to face us: 'No, Ciccio, I need you here with me to help me unpack.'

And like a pet puppy dog, Ciccio turns on his tail and follows his master, leaving me alone and disappointed. I would never dare say it to anyone around here – not Mamma or Mena or Ciccio – but sometimes I don't know if I really like Signor Edoardo.

14

Do I Want to Die?

As I woke in my cousin Marianna's single bed in her tiny but cosy bedroom, my eyes instinctively flitted to the shuttered window and the majestic view of the rolling, deep-blue Ionian Sea that lay hidden behind it. At sunrise it looks like the sea is on fire. On a very clear day, I could see the coast of mainland Italy opposite, and even in the depths of my misery, it never failed to bring a weak smile to my pasty face. Who wouldn't love to start the day with that view?

It was one I'd become used to over the past three months, because I'd never left the room in that time except to visit the bathroom. The traumas and burdens of the past few years had finally taken their toll on my own health, physically and mentally. But once again, Zia Mena was there to catch me when I'd fallen.

After returning from Australia, I moved back into The Cave with Edoardo, but he soon qualified as an economist and had to move to Catania to find work. Worried about my health, which hadn't been good for some time, he arranged for me to move into Zia Mena's house until I was properly back on my feet.

My problems started with me losing weight for no apparent reason and catching any bug that was going around. My good friend and doctor Luca put it down to stress and my immune system being low. Well, nobody could say I hadn't had a stressful time, even though I thought I'd coped with it well. Not so apparently.

I started feeling really ill completely out of the blue. I had a sky-high temperature and what seemed to be flu symptoms like I'd never known before. I couldn't even get out of bed without fainting, and my raging temperature refused to go down. As the days passed, I became weaker and weaker, and soon stopped eating altogether. Luca would come every morning to check my blood pressure in the hope of any improvement. When none came, I was taken to Zia Mena's.

But despite all her loving care, things went from bad to worse and I began to feel as if I was fading away. I was permanently exhausted, and it was as if I was feeling nothing. I had no will left and no desire to get better.

At times, I began to see myself from the outside, as if I was having an out-of-body experience. It was as if it wasn't my own body, and at just thirty-five kilos, around five stone, it didn't look anything like it either. Only in my early twenties, I was wasting away and frightening everyone around me. Zia Mena cried every time she left my room, as did Rocco, who was a regular visitor and spent hours there holding my hand in silence. My brother didn't know what to say or do anymore. Nobody did. Yet, I didn't care about what I was doing to them.

Suddenly, I heard footsteps and I could hear Luca talking to my aunt and Edoardo outside my room. I paid little attention to what they were saying, but I did hear Zia Mena bursting into tears just before Luca walked into the room. For once, he didn't have his doctor's bag and he didn't make any attempt to check my blood pressure. He just stood and stared at me without speaking a word, with a very stern look on his face.

Then all of a sudden, he said, 'Right! Today is the last day I will come to see you. Frankly, I have better things to do than watch you die. Do you want to die? Fine by me. But I don't want to see your aunt and brother distraught, day in and day out, because of your selfishness. Don't you think they've already been through enough? Don't you think losing your mum was bad enough, without having to see you giving up and disappearing in front of their eyes? There is nothing I or anyone else can do to help you unless you want us to. That is all I have to say. Goodbye!'

With that, he turned on his heel and left. Just like that. I doubt I would have said anything in reply, but he didn't even give me the chance. Shock therapy. His last attempt to save me, and I'm happy to say he succeeded. I was definitely shocked by it, and being shocked was a sort of feeling, after being numb for so long.

Then something started to bother me over the next few days. But what was it?

I wasn't particularly bothered about dying or Luca not coming to see me again. Slowly, it registered. Of course – it was when he talked about Zia Mena and Edoardo not deserving to see me like this that something had clicked inside me. I was hurt. For the first time in what felt like a very long time, I felt pain, shame and sadness. How could I do this to them? I of all people should have known the pain I was causing them. What would my mum say if she saw what I was doing?

After that, little by little, I came out of my near-vegetative state and started asking for food. My aunt would cook me a meal, like a fillet steak of the best beef she could find, and cut in tiny portions that gradually became bigger and then eventually normal bite sizes. It was like weaning a baby. Two of the people who had become really good friends since my return, Iris and Ilaria, came to visit often, and they took me out for my first outing. Again, like eating, I had to do it little by little, step by step, and every time I made it a little bit further.

I was very frail and it was a long recovery, but with Luca's medical help, Zia Mena's continued love and care, Edoardo and my friends, I eventually recovered.

Sadly, my father never visited me once. To give him the benefit of the doubt, maybe that was because he had fallen out with

Zia Mena. Although I doubt she would have refused him if he'd really wanted to visit. No matter the circumstances, she always said, 'He is still your father.'

Whatever, one thing was now abundantly clear: I had a second chance and I had to take it. This meant I had to make some radical changes in my life. Leave the past behind. That meant my on-off relationship with Rocco, or anyone else for that matter, had to end. For good. I had to start afresh and concentrate on myself. A new, clean break.

Soon there was light at the end of the tunnel. With Iris and Ilaria, I formed a new circle of friends. There were about ten of us, and Iris, Ilaria and I were the only girls in the group. We were all single and all good pals. I'm sure some of the boys wanted more than that, and the occasional casual fling happened, but we managed to keep the group together without too much drama. It was as if I was finally living all those teenage years that I'd lost, without a care in the world.

I did casual jobs – mostly seasonal positions. I worked as a shop assistant, on information desks and I also babysat. One job was working at the Greek-Roman Theatre as a hostess – and yes, we do indeed have a Greek-Roman theatre in Taormina. Perched on a rocky outcrop, the ancient theatre looms over Taormina and is still used for performances to this day, its acoustics working as well now as when it was first built in the third century BC. With its impressive natural setting, splendid view towards the Calabrian coast, the Ionian coast of Sicily and the spectacular Mount Etna in the background, this theatre in one of Sicily's main attractions. Hostesses were girls who led people to their seats – 'usherettes' in England.

Iris was a hostess like me, and we had the most amazing time. We watched concerts, operas, plays and ballets, and as we only worked evenings, we had all day to go to the beach. After work, normally around midnight, we would get changed and then go out for a meal and meet the others in our group. Taormina seemed the most beautiful place to be. In summer in

Sicily, every night of the week is a night out, and we managed to get by with very little sleep for a long time. What a joy to be young and free.

Midweek outings varied from pizzas somewhere, followed by a nightclub – usually Septimo or Tout Va – or a bonfire on the beach with a night dip in the sea, or a ride on motorbikes. It could simply be a *passeggiata* and a drink in the Corso Umberto. But one of my fondest memories is of the cosy evenings at al Cavalluccio Marino, my friend Lorenzo's beach house. We would all get together and take food, very often fish caught by one of the guys or *ricci di mare* – sea urchins. I love *ricci di mare* to this day. We spent many happy evenings there, eating, drinking, playing music, singing and playing silly games. Just being happy. *So happiness does exist*, I thought.

We established a going-out routine, a weekend ritual. Friday night was reserved for Il Pigalle, an unpretentious club with good music, cheap entrance fees and drinks, and a very interesting mix of people. It was some forty minutes away from Taormina, so up to seven of us would all clamber into whatever car was available to get there. Saturdays, without fail, were reserved for La Giara, an upmarket, private club in Taormina's historical centre and also the title of a play by my favourite playwright, Luigi Pirandello. We would dress up to the nines to gain entrance and more often than not we wangled our way in without paying, as Lorenzo was the son of the town's mayor, which basically guaranteed us free entry to the places we visited to dance into the early hours.

Sunday was the *perroquet* night. Taormina had a large gay community, and every Sunday evening, men dressed as glamorous drag queens would put on shows, singing, dancing and interacting with an animated audience. It was a bit like a scene from the film *Birdcage* and it was so much fun. Every Sunday the club was packed with people of all ages, sexual orientations and classes. It always struck me as strange that such an open-minded town, that now had no problem tolerating homosexuality, had forced my wonderful gay cousin Mattia to leave Taormina in the late seventies to work in the north of Italy because he couldn't bear to bring shame on his family.

Wherever we went out to at night, we never forgot to take our sunglasses, as we normally ended up eating hot croissants fresh from the local baker's oven in front of a stunning dawn sunrise. With every passing day for two years, I was feeling stronger and more confident. By twenty-five, I finally felt carefree and less bothered about what the future might hold for me – until late one afternoon at the beginning of August 1993.

I was at the beach. The sun wasn't as strong, and there was a light, warm breeze that made the hot Sicilian summer days a little bit more bearable. I was happily sitting with my group of friends, relaxing and chatting after a day in the sea. My skin was still hot and slightly reddened by the scorching sun, but I didn't have a care in the world. For me this socialising was still a novelty, and I was relishing every single moment of my belated youth.

Suddenly, one of my friends pointed at a little red dot moving in the middle of the sea and said, 'Michele is coming.'

I had absolutely no idea who Michele was, which was quite strange, considering what a small place Taormina is.

Slowly but steadily, the little red dot got closer and bigger, and as it came into focus, I could see it was a canoe. Once it had reached the shore, a tall, tanned, muscular, green-eyed guy stepped out and joined us. Everyone greeted him, as they all seemed to know him except me. Michele had a very relaxed air about him, soft-spoken and calm. Sitting down, he started chatting, and at some point he looked at me and smiled. Suddenly my stomach was doing somersaults!

The following weekend started as usual at Il Pigalle on Friday. Michele had agreed to come with us, which made me feel strangely pleased and excited. What should I wear? High heels? Yes, definitely high heels as he was so tall. Smart? Not too smart, as I didn't want him to think I'd made too much of an effort. *Oh my God, this is nerve-racking! I haven't done this in such a long time. What if he doesn't like me?*

But I needn't have worried, as that same evening our chats turned to kisses and we immediately became an item. Soon we were inseparable. We spent the next two weeks together, every single day, trying not to think about him going back to England at the end of the summer, where he was working in the hotel sector. *It's a summer fling, that's all,* I kept repeating to myself. *Don't get too involved; don't fall in love. Just enjoy the moment. You deserve it.*

The two weeks came to an end and Michele went back to England. Neither of us really knew what to say, but he was clearly as upset and confused as I was.

'Let's keep in touch,' he mumbled eventually.

Neither of us quite understood how we could get so close in such a short time, and I was left trying to go back to my life with an overwhelming feeling of sadness. Maybe it really was a fling. After all, I couldn't see how it could ever work. He belonged to a family of hotel owners in Taormina, and his work in a five-star hotel in London was part of his training, so that one day he could take over the reins of their empire. After London it would be Vienna for two years, then the United States. I couldn't even begin to comprehend how I could fit into these rigid plans.

Happily, Michele had only been gone a week when I received a phone call saying he was coming back for another fortnight. I couldn't believe my luck. Everything was pointing towards the possibility that he was actually coming back for me, but I didn't dare hope too much. Was I worth it? Would somebody do that for me? Go the extra mile? Somebody new, fresh. The future – nothing to do with the past.

After his return, everything went really fast, and by the end of August he was asking me to move in with him in London. Head over heels in love by this stage, I agreed! Love really did exist. That mad, irrational, inexplicable feeling that makes you do things you never thought you would do! I was hooked and I loved the idea of being 'in love'.

Although the thought of London was as terrifying as it was exciting, what did I really have to keep me in Taormina? All that mattered was that I would be with him, even though I had no idea what work I was going to do there or how I would support myself. Michele was working on a hotel reception desk, a job set up for him by his uncle, but I had no such luxury. Still, nothing mattered. I was going and anyway, I only thought I would be away for a few months, maybe until summer. Improve my English, then come home, find a job. All I had to do was tell Zia Mena and Edoardo.

Zia Mena was actually very forward-thinking and support- ive. After all, her husband had worked away on a cruise liner, her son lived in the north of Italy and her daughter, though still in Sicily, lived about an hour away from Taormina. In her mind, leaving was the only thing to do to succeed, and she was right.

I introduced her to Michele and told her we would be living in a flat together. She didn't ask any questions, but I knew she'd chosen to believe that we would have two separate bedrooms. In her world, it was absolutely unimaginable that we could share a bed. Although she knew we were boyfriend and girlfriend, she wanted to believe that we had a platonic relationship until he made an honest woman out of me and married me in a Catholic church. Who was I to upset and disrespect her beliefs? Edoardo accepted my decision – he only ever wanted what was best for me. I didn't even tell my father.

All my friends had bets that I wouldn't last long in England, which they could only envisage as a cold, grey, foggy country, hence the rainbow-coloured sweater they bought me for a leav- ing present to remember them by. How would I live without my sea and the sun?

Quite honestly, it barely crossed my mind. I just knew I had to go and be with Michele to prove myself. To live, not die, as I had come so perilously close to doing.

15
Hello, London!

Stepping off the plane and onto the airport tarmac, my first impression of England was that it was indeed cold, grey and gloomy. Nothing like the warm, sunny September day I had left behind in Sicily a few hours earlier.

Hey-ho, let's not judge a book by its cover. Soon I would be with Michele again, and as I entered the arrivals lounge, there he was waiting for me with a calm, pleased smile on his face. All fears and doubts melted away the instant I was back in his arms.

For the first couple of days, we barely left the flat he was renting in Walthamstow and we spent most of the time just enjoying being back together. When we eventually ventured out, Michele suggested we visit his landlady, Aida, at her house. 'She can't wait to meet you,' he reassured me.

Although I didn't know Aida, who coincidentally was from Taormina, I knew her nephew. Just knowing that she was from my home town gave me a warm feeling of comfort and security, and I decided that I liked her already.

A very good-looking young Italian man in his twenties, who I soon discovered was Aida's son Raffaele, opened the door, and as we entered I smelled the familiar aroma of tomato sauce.

'Ragu!' I exclaimed excitedly.

On the kitchen floor, a little boy crawled and played as Aida came towards me with a huge friendly smile.

'Welcome to Londra, Beatrice, *che piacere conoscerti finalmente* – what a pleasure to meet you at last! You look just like your mum,' she said, hugging me like she had always known me. I loved the fact that she'd known my mother, and I politely asked if the little boy was her son.

'Whaaaat?' she replies. 'This is Chris, my daughter's son – my grandson! I am way too old to be his mother!' She laughed out loud.

We all laughed along with her, and if there was any ice to break, it smashed in that instant. She didn't look too old to be his mother to me. There was something so young about Aida: her energy, her willingness to enjoy life to the full. It made her seem young, helped along with the fact that she actually looked great for her age.

Immediately, I felt a connection with her and trusted her as she took me under her wing, guiding me through all the everyday challenges I had to face in this strange country. She took me to the best supermarkets, showing me where to find various things; she came with me to register with a local GP surgery and escorted me to get my English National Insurance number. Anything I needed, emotionally or materially, she was there for me, and I soon grew to love her as a substitute mother, older sister and friend.

In turn, I was welcomed into her family like one of her own – *la figlia adottiva*, the adopted daughter. She became my rock, and Sunday lunch at her place became as sacred for me as attending Mass is for a devout Catholic. I never missed it unless I absolutely had to.

Everything that I was doing, Aida had done forty years earlier, aged eighteen and pregnant, with a husband who left at the crack of dawn to work as a restaurant chef, only returning late at night. She had no support, and they lived in a one-room bedsit with a stove and a shared bathroom on a different floor.

In order to get married, Aida and her husband had chosen *la fuitina*, which literally means 'sudden escape'. It was a ritual then common in Sicily whereby a young couple would elope to marry if it was against the wishes of their family or they couldn't afford a proper wedding. Their absence – normally a few days – would imply that sexual intercourse had taken place, forcing families to consent to a *matrimonio riparatorio* – a shotgun wedding to 'repair' the damage occurred. Zia Mena and her husband were two more of many of that generation to have done this, and I'm sure that in some small villages it still happens today.

I quickly discovered that Aida is one of the strongest people I know, certainly one of those that I respect the most, and she remains one of the dearest people in my life. Always making herself available to anyone who needs her, she has helped a long list of Italians that moved to England. I wasn't the only one by any means. Sometimes I wonder where she found the energy to work, look after a house, children, grandchildren and us – the lost Italian kids.

After a two-week honeymoon period with Michele, I started thinking about work. With few contacts and relevant qualifications, I quickly realised that my job options were limited and I would need to start at the very bottom of the career ladder. I settled for a job as an au pair for the first six months, but when I saw an advert for a receptionist role in a very posh five-star hotel in Mayfair, I decided I was going to apply, even if my chances of getting it were limited.

'Don't bother. You'll never get it,' was Michele's *helpful* advice.

'Oh,' I replied, quite surprised and deflated by his attitude.

Aida, who could always be relied on for positive support, took a different stance, persuading me that nothing ventured meant nothing gained. I applied for the job anyway and somehow landed an interview.

Still affected by Michele's negativity though, I didn't even make much of an effort dressing up for it, as I was so sure I was wasting my time. After all, Michele knew the industry. Maybe he was right and I should have been applying for work as a chambermaid, dishwasher or waitress.

Yet somehow, against all the odds, I was offered the job. I was convinced that the kindly interviewer felt sorry for me and wanted to give me a chance, but why I got it was irrelevant really. I had the job!

As much as I couldn't believe my good fortune, neither could Michele. 'You won't last more than a week,' he predicted.

But I was determined to prove him wrong, and at the end of my first day there, my manager Lorraine called me into her office and in her lovely, warm Scottish accent she said, 'I hope you had a good first shift, Beatrice. See you tomorrow, and thank you.'

'Thank you?' I replied, slightly confused. 'For what?'

Smiling, she looked at me and said, 'For doing such a great job today!'

Somewhat stunned, I couldn't believe I was being thanked just for doing what I was being paid to do. It was such an alien concept to me, as in Sicily you were expected to consider yourself lucky that you even had a job. I held that position for two whole years, and throughout that time, Lorraine said thank you at the end of every shift.

Looking back, I do wonder why Michele couldn't have had more belief in me. Maybe his male pride made him jealous. I never found out though, as Vienna came calling for him but not me. To complete his international training, he needed to move on again, and it became clear that there was no place in his plans for me, so we split up. Even with Aida's unfailing love and support, London was still a lonely place for a young Italian girl struggling to get by on her own, so with a broken heart (mostly from the realisation that the relationship hadn't been what I'd hoped for), I made the decision to return to sunny Sicily.

Reluctantly, I moved in with my father and Petronilla, as Edoardo had built bridges with them and he was living there at the time. I guess he'd had enough of living on his own in The

Cave (which he'd kept for weekends in Taormina after moving to Catania). It wasn't an ideal arrangement, but in truth I had little choice.

It was perfectly cordial, and we all remained distantly polite to each other. I immediately began looking for a permanent job. I imagined that with all my experience in London, I wouldn't have any problem finding employment in the hotel or tourism industry in my own country.

How wrong I was. I'd forgotten how the system works in my motherland, where nothing could ever be achieved without recommendations from somebody with influence. I had to rely on my old contacts to find enough occasional temporary work to keep me while I searched for a permanent position in a hotel or elsewhere in the hospitality sector.

Opening any doors soon proved to be a struggle. As I trekked around, leaving my CV in several hotels, it dawned on me that once I'd walked out the door, it would be dumped straight in the bin. Even if a job became available, which in itself was unlikely as local people tend to hang on to secure employment until they retire, there would be various *raccomandati*, recommended people, waiting to step into those newly vacated shoes. Even if the people had no relevant qualifications or experience.

Realising that despite all my hard work and experience, I didn't have a chance in that small-minded town, it became clear that Taormina wasn't the place for me anymore and I was reminded why I'd left in the first place. It was nothing new really. Had I not always felt like a bit of an outcast here, always wanting different things? I wanted to travel and see the world.

Facing the fact that my prospects were bleak, I instinctively knew that my next move should be to return to England, where I had quietly been growing in confidence and self-worth due to being appreciated for my hard work and talent.

Even though my relationship with Michele had soured, I have to give him credit for changing my life forever. It may not have been the great everlasting love affair we'd thought we had, but I'll always have him to thank for helping me break free from Taormina. My golden prison. I had escaped once with his support, and I could do it again alone this time.

So, picking up the phone, the first person I called was Aida to tell her my decision and ask if I could stay with her while resettling myself with a home and a job. Overjoyed to hear my news, her answer was 'yes, of course'. She had missed her adopted daughter and suggested I call Lorraine next to see if I could have my old job back. Reluctantly, I did, but all the while a little doubting voice in my head was asking, *Why would she do that for me?*

Lorraine didn't give me my old job back – she gave me a better one. I wasn't returning as a receptionist but as a shift manager. Surprised, scared, nervous and full of hope, I booked the first flight out and cried all the way back to London.

16

Return of the Prodigal Daughter

Before I knew it, I was living in Aida's familiar house, back in my seat at the dinner table, eating her delicious home-cooked Italian food. It was as if I'd never been away. I slipped straight into my new role at the Mayfair hotel without a hitch. So far, so good. However, at age twenty-eight, I knew I couldn't take refuge at Aida's forever. After three happy months there, it was time for me to spread my wings. As long as they didn't spread too far. It was very important to me that I could still make it back to Aida's for Sunday lunch every week, work permitting.

I started scanning all the accommodation ads in the local papers and newsagents' windows and eventually I found a room in a nearby shared house and hesitantly made an appointment to view it. I had never lived with strangers before and was nervous about who I might be sharing with. But I needn't have worried. The two girls already living there – Maeve from Dublin and Naomi from Liverpool – couldn't have been lovelier and it was soon the start of a fabulous friendship. For me, that flat at 113 Forest Road will always represent another new beginning. Fun and freedom!

My new flatmates took it upon themselves to educate me about the English way of life, which was quite an eye-opener for me. When I had been in London previously with Michele, I hadn't absorbed any English culture. We'd lived our lives as we would have in Sicily, socialising only with other Italians and rarely going out of the flat.

But if I had any notions of my flatmates introducing me to genteel afternoon teas and cucumber sandwiches, I could forget them. This was more about going to the pub and downing pints of beer while nibbling on packets of crisps and peanuts! It was exactly the same when I went out with friends and colleagues from work. Never a big drinker, the 'rounds' system meant that I usually had full glasses lined up in front of me by the end of the evening. But they persisted with my *training* and it wasn't long before I could drink three pints of Guinness without flinching. When the scales and the waistband of my hotel uniform began to show the results of this, though, I realised there had to be a healthier way of having fun that was more me.

In return for Maeve and Naomi's *cultural education*, I was already practising my culinary skills on them. My guinea pigs. I was happy to cook traditional Italian food, and they were just as happy to eat anything I put in front of them. So I decided to bring more Italian traditions into our social life and started organising dinner parties, with lots of drinks still but with equal amounts of good food to soak up the alcohol.

Some Sicilian friends were guests at one dinner party, and one of them, Iris, who had played such an important role in my life after my illness, was shocked to witness my new-found drinking ability. To celebrate, we kept drinking tequila until I completely blacked out, unable later to remember a thing. Maeve later told me that she'd found me with my head down the toilet being terribly sick. I had also fallen down the stairs. Perhaps it was time for me to rethink my new social habits. Slowly, I realised that I could still go out – or stay in – and have fun without having to keep up with everyone else's drinking. I accepted my limits and slowed down on the alcohol. It was a good arrangement.

Ever keen to improve myself, I quickly realised that the great thing about the UK – which was very different from Sicily – was that if you're ambitious and you have the will, you can move on. So when the time was right, I left my job at the hotel to work in a private travel agency owned by Mr LoCascio, a Sicilian guy, in King's Cross. While there, I signed up for a professional course to qualify as a travel agent and made new Italian friends – Francesca, Serena and Grazia – who became a big part of my new life in London. Francesca and I in particular hit it off immediately as our boss became the subject of elaborate teasing and endless laughs.

'It is not six yet, girls. Make sure you finish all the tickets for tomorrow,' Mr LoCascio would bark at us, sensing we were already making plans for the evening involving Caffrey's Irish Ale and chips!

'We've done everything, Mr LoCascio, don't worry,' we would reply.

'Well, I do worry. I have to worry – I am the owner of this place. And someone has to worry, since you obviously don't care,' he would chunter on in his heavily accented English.

Francesca had arrived in London with a degree in languages from Catania University but zero English conversation skills. At her university, reading *Beowulf* had been considered more important than speaking to people. She told me that during her first six months in London she had avidly reread Agatha Christie novels, bought for 10p each from a stall in Portobello Market, and watched TV with a vacant gaze, trying to grasp some meaning – any meaning in fact – and often misinterpreting it. Then one evening, while watching *Inspector Morse*, suddenly everything clicked. She found that she could finally make sense of the English language. All had become clear. After that, she convinced herself that her best English teachers had been not her university lecturers, but Agatha Christie and John Thaw.

Unlike me, with my long, wavy jet-black hair, olive complexion and elongated dark eyes, Francesca had fair hair and a pale complexion, so there was nothing typically Sicilian about her, apart from her minuscule height perhaps. In love with England, its culture and lifestyle, she was determined to fit in and was trying to forget her origins altogether, whereas I was always quick to point out my Mediterranean origins with pride. Her English accent was perfect, while I had, and still have, a strong Italian accent.

I had decided early on to focus on perfecting my grammar rather than my pronunciation. It may sound silly, but I cling to my Italian accent, as it's another part of my heritage and identity. In truth, we both cared little about the past at that time, as we were too focused on the present and what the future might have in store for us.

Working at the travel agency was fun. The money was laughable, but we got by. Francesca was studying part-time for a degree in literature to make up for her lack of fulfilment, as she clung to the belief that she was destined for better things than working for an Italian travel agency in London. She was cynical, a bit of an intellectual snob nurturing high aspirations, but also very funny and self-deprecating. I was more practical and focused on gaining qualifications in the business I was learning the ropes of. Despite our differences, a strong, lasting friendship was forming, and whenever Francesca got a new job, she managed to persuade her bosses to give me a chance there soon afterwards. In fact, she did that on three separate occasions.

My next role was with a French tour operator, which indulged my desire to travel, and over the next two years I was lucky enough to visit Polynesia, Thailand and the Caribbean, among other exotic destinations. I was in my element, meeting so many people from so many backgrounds and cultures, making my life so much richer. One of the best holidays I ever had was visiting a friend of a French friend in South Africa, and I can proudly say that I had a boyfriend who hailed from the Australian city of Wagga Wagga. Impossible to forget where he came from!

Despite all the fun, there were still downs in my London life, and when Maeve and Naomi decided to return to their home towns, it was time for me to leave our Forest Road house. Sadly, it coincided with a few of my Italian friends leaving too.

Serena left first to look after her grandmother and then Iris, followed shortly afterwards by Achille, her talented musician boyfriend who had livened up our dinner parties with his guitar. There was nothing he couldn't play, although from his extensive repertoire, his rendition of the Sicilian folk song 'Ciuri Ciuri' remained the dearest to me. Iris and Achille's presence at our dinner parties was always a reminder of my origins. The two never turned up without bringing a huge amount of food either. I can still taste the *sasizza* – Sicilian sausages – we ate one New Year's Eve. In the days before cheap international flights, I could only afford to visit Taormina once a year, so in between these times they brought home to me.

Without my close friends, I had to move into another rented room in another house, and once again I landed well. My new landlady, Abebi, became another great source of support. Born in Nigeria, she had moved to England with her parents when very young, and as we talked about our different cultures, we discovered that we had a lot of things in common and formed a strong bond. Families, we realised, played an important role in both our cultures.

Never was that brought home to me more than the day on which my brother Edoardo's daughter – my beautiful niece Atena – was born in 1999. Thankfully, her early years coincided with the launch of cheap airlines and I was able to visit her more often than my salary would have previously allowed. As a result, a close aunt-and-niece bond was formed.

Atena brought me such immense joy and hope for the future; I loved her as I would love my own daughter. Her arrival meant that our small family, for all its past problems, would live on, and as a Sicilian woman, that continuation of our bloodline was very important to me. As I hurtled towards my mid-thirties, I was painfully aware that my biological clock was stubbornly ticking. I was beginning to seriously doubt that I would ever be lucky enough to settle down with the right man and have a family of my own to love.

*View of Taormina from Giardini Naxos Port – Taormina
(from the Malambrì Archive)*

*Greek Roman Theatre with Mount Etna in the background –
Taormina (from the Malambrì Archive)*

Woman overlooking Isola Bella – Taormina (from the Malambrì Archive)

Taormina Cathedral – Taormina (from the Malambrì Archive)

A boy photographed by Wilhelm von Gloeden – Taormina
(from the Malambrì Archive)

A girl photographed by Wilhelm von Gloeden – Taormina
(from the Malambrì Archive)

Boy on a donkey – Taormina (from the Malambrì Archive)

*Postcard of Taormina featuring a traditional Sicilian cart with
Mount Etna in the background*

Cheapside – London

Royal Albert Hall – London

Houses of Parliament – London

Kensington Gardens – London

17

Wedding Bells

Padre Giovanni
(Priest of Santa Caterina Church. Taormina. 10 January 1959)

No matter how many times I have witnessed it during my many years in Taormina, the spectacular sight of the sun setting over Mount Etna never fails to amaze me. On this chilly winter's evening, I'm as enthralled by it as ever. The snow on top of our unpredictable volcano looks like flames against the orange-tinted blue sky. God's own handiwork in all its kaleidoscopic splendour.

It is especially good to go to bed this evening having seen this view, as tomorrow is the tenth of January, the day I have the privilege of marrying Signor Edoardo's 'adopted' son Ciccio and Linetta, the younger daughter of his former head cook at Villa Sole, the late Maria Greco. It's as if God is reminding me that I have made the right decision in accepting the Baron's surprise invitation to officiate at their nuptials, even if I was rather baffled as to why he asked me to do so and not Monsignore Aspidi.

Given the elevated status of the bride and groom, brought about by their close association with Signor Edoardo, it would have been more appropriate. Certainly, the snub didn't go down well with the Monsignor, whose nose, shall we say, has been put rather firmly out of joint by this hierarchical disregard. But as long as God is approving, why should I worry? There is quite enough for me to focus on at the moment. Maybe I should pour myself another cup of hot canarino – a drink made with lemon zest and bay leaves – to warm me up. It's good for digestion and will help me have a good night's sleep.

Tomorrow I must face the task in hand. Signor Edoardo and I have been firm friends for a long time now, I am proud to say, and I don't want to let him down on this important occasion. At seventy-one, his health is already failing fast and who knows how many more events of this magnitude he will witness in his life-time. I say 'magnitude' but maybe that's the wrong word, given that this wedding has had to be scaled down somewhat drastically.

Originally the plan was to hold it in the summer months in *la cattedrale*, the cathedral, with a huge, lavish celebration afterwards for a multitude of guests of varying importance. But as Signor Edoardo became sicker by the week, it was decided to bring it forward and hold a much smaller, low-key reception for family and a few close friends only.

To suit this intimate ceremony, they have chosen a historic church that fits it perfectly. Chiesa Madonna della Rocca (Church of the Madonna of the Rock) is a very modest and rustic little chapel carved into rock at the top of Mount Tauro, overlooking Taormina. There is also a Saracen castle close by. The site has the same stunning views over Mount Etna and the sea that I enjoy from my own humble abode. It even has an important legend attached to it.

Apparently, one day a young shepherd boy was feeding his flock on the mountain when a sudden storm forced him to take refuge in a nearby cave with his sheep. As the storm worsened and lightning forked in the sky above him, he was terrified. At that point, a beautiful lady dressed in blue comforted him and reassured him that the sun would appear soon.

When the storm ended, the boys' parents launched a search and found him near the castle rocks, sitting peacefully surrounded by his protective flock. The boy told them what he had witnessed and it attracted widespread local attention. Visitors noticed that there was an impression of the Madonna figure on the rock, where the shepherd boy had seen the vision. After the Bishop was notified of this miracle, he had a church built there using the stone of the cave. Beside it they built a large concrete cross, which dominates the whole of Taormina and is visible from all sides.

Well, enough of my musings. I must go to bed now – early start for me tomorrow. I need to get to the church before anyone else and check everything is in order.

The morning after, on arrival at the chapel, I am not disappointed. What a perfect setting for a happy wedding day! Had the event gone as originally planned, it would have been impossible to hold it here, as the chapel is far too small to accommodate a large gathering. Inside the dark building, it is pleasant to see that it has been brightened with small bouquets of yellow tulips, Linetta's favourite flowers, and small white roses.

Although blessed with wealth since she became engaged to Ciccio, Linetta has always maintained a very modest attitude to life. *Na brava carusa piddaveru* – A very good girl indeed. She is a genuinely good young woman who's been looking after Signor Edoardo with great kindness and compassion since he's needed assistance. I myself have been praying for my good friend every day, as I have this morning. May he be well enough to enjoy this special day to celebrate the union of such a fine young couple.

Both of the betrothed are blessed with such good looks, they complement each other perfectly – even resembling actors from the old black-and-white movies shown at the Cinema Olimpia. I don't doubt for a moment that this match was instigated by the Baron, who has never wanted anything but the best for Ciccio. He must realise that as a bride, Linetta provides nothing less.

Just before 10.30 a.m. it's time for two of my altar boys and myself to take up our post at the entrance to welcome our guests. Linetta's family start to arrive; first her sisters Mena and Amalia, the eldest, with her own young family, and their father Beppe, who is blind and in need of assistance.

'Accomodatevi e benvenuti – Come in and welcome! The front row of seats on the right of the altar are waiting for you. Signor Edoardo and the groom's family will be on the left. The cushion placed there is for Signor Edoardo.'

Here he is, being helped out of the car by Ciccio. How sad it is to see him so stooped and struggling even with his ivory-and-gold walking cane as he proudly makes his way to the entrance. Ciccio's mother Concetta and two of his sisters follow in his unsteady path.

Around thirty guests arrive altogether and are ushered inside. Then we're treated to the arrival of the bride in a show-stopping Ferrari 250 Europa specially hired for the day. It is the motor that Ciccio aspires to own in the future. Linetta looks radiant as she steps out, happy to be marrying her childhood sweetheart – the boy she first loved at just thirteen and has grown up with.

Now twenty-four, she is about to become Signora Curcurace and her future is as bright as the long rose-gold chain around her neck. A present from Signor Edoardo, it was the chain of his pocket watch, a token of his esteem for this young woman here today. She looks so elegant in her simply styled white silk muslin dress. A full tulle veil, embellished with a white satin bow, tumbles around her shoulders, complementing perfectly her olive skin and jet-black hair.

At the entrance, supported by Mena, Beppe is waiting to take Linetta's hand, and together they walk down the aisle. Such a shame her mother, who died when Linetta was just thirteen, can't be here with them. Even though Beppe can't see his beautiful daughter, at least he's here with her to mark the occasion. And what a happy relief it must be for him to know that she has such a financially secure future and he no longer has to worry about her.

Looking very dapper in his dark blue two-piece suit, Ciccio looks at his radiant bride as she walks towards him and smiles.

The ceremony goes smoothly, despite my nerves that I wouldn't perform as well as the Monsignor might have, and the bride and groom lead the way to Villa Sole for the reception, laughing as they dodge the rice thrown by well-wishers.

A long table covered in a white linen cloth groans under the weight of the cold buffet. Linetta has insisted on cooking every dish, with her sisters' help – typical Sicilian starters and fish-based dishes – and it looks delicious. The abundance of rich white and red wine washes them down very nicely as a band made up of locals plays in the background. Like her mother, Linetta is a great cook and has been feeding Signor Edoardo since her mother's death. The only addition to today's wedding feast that she hasn't created herself, I believe, is the two-tier sponge wedding cake made of *panna, crema pasticcera e fragoline di bosco* – whipped cream, custard cream and fresh wild strawberries.

The numerous orange and lemon trees are heaving with fruit, and combined with the wedding decorations – the strings of white roses and fairy lights – they create the perfect backdrop for the event. Such a shame that the black-and-white wedding photographs won't capture the spectacular array of nature's colours here, set against the bright blue sky.

Sadly, it is soon all too much for Signor Edoardo and he has to retire early, exhausted yet happy in the knowledge that his Ciccio is in safe hands in the house he has had built for them behind Villa Sole. He really couldn't have done more for this fine young couple to ensure their future together is a long and happy one. May God be with them every step of the way in this exciting new chapter of their lives.

18

A Good Husband

It was Saturday, 17 May 2003, and I was sitting in a beautiful silver-blue wedding dress next to my new husband at our wedding reception in a Lake District hotel. I was waiting for my brother to stand up and make a speech in front of our hundred guests. Knowing the limitations of Edoardo's English and aware that he had no written notes to rely on, I felt naturally nervous for him before all these people, mainly strangers to him. But I needn't have worried. Right on cue, he stood up, calmly put his hands on the table, looked down and paused slightly before speaking.

'Today is a good day,' he began. 'My sister, my only family, is marrying Richard. I met him just a few times, but I know Richard is a good, good man. I know our mother looks down in this moment and she smiles. I am very happy. Thank you.'

Suddenly everybody was on their feet, clapping loud and long. Heartfelt. Like me, people were wiping tears from their faces, until my cousin Stefano broke the mood.

'Edoardo!' he shouted. 'You are beautiful!'

A huge laugh erupted out en masse, lightening the ambience of our special day surrounded by loved ones. Only my father was missing. His name was even left off the wedding certificate. I was still angry and unable to forgive him for the way he'd treated our mother and his subsequent callous behaviour towards Edoardo and me. He was a poor husband and a poor father. But I had chosen differently, and I was determined that he wasn't going to spoil my special day. The one for which I'd been hoping and waiting for such a very long time. The one I feared I might never see.

I first met Richard O'Sullivan when I changed jobs to earn more money so that I could save up enough to move to Barcelona with two of my good friends. Why not? I loved the Spanish city, and moving on seemed the right thing to do at that point of my life. My on-off relationship with my Australian boyfriend had ended when he returned Down Under. My friend Francesca was leaving her job as PA to the managing director of an American media research company and asked if I was interested. As it was much better pay, I said yes, planning to stay for only a year and learn Spanish while saving for my next move.

I got the job and quickly settled in at the prestigious offices in Piccadilly Circus. The atmosphere was laid-back and the job straightforward enough, with an easy-going boss and little stress. Richard worked there as a research analyst on a different floor, so our paths didn't cross at first. It was only later that he told me he'd noticed me in my first week at a conference we'd both attended, and had asked who the pretty Indian girl was. Indian? In turn, I mistakenly thought he was gay after being fed duff info from Francesca, who'd misread his naturally kind, gentle nature. As time went on, we moved offices and were working on the same floor during a particularly hot, sticky summer.

'Can I please have a jacuzzi under my desk?' Richard joked as he passed my desk.

'Leave it to me – I'll look into it,' I replied.

The ice was broken, and I registered the fact that he was funny but had a terrible dress sense! Maybe I was a bit too harsh on him, but I couldn't help it. Blame my innate Italian feel for fashion. From then on, we started going out for lunches and drinks together and shared banter in the office. Knowing him better, but still thinking he was gay, I opened up and confessed that I was ready to settle down and that all I wanted was a family.

'Me too,' he replied to my surprise, as I knew he was into the dance-music scene and spent every weekend clubbing.

On a later occasion at a Turkish restaurant, which turned out to be our first date, Richard, a vegetarian, watched me tuck into a huge mixed grill. During our conversation, I blurted out, 'Am I ever going to meet a nice man in this country who wants what I want?'

Surprised by my question, he decided to take it as a challenge. Even when I returned from Sardinia, babbling on about a fisherman friend of a friend that I'd met, he kept asking me out so I thought I'd better confirm that he really was gay. A colleague I asked soon set me straight and I started panicking. I began to think that all the things I'd said would give him the wrong impression and I needed to discourage him. As much as I liked him – he was funny, clever, motivated and very kind – I just saw him as a friend. Being younger than me and into dance music, we led such different lives that it would surely never work.

Well, whatever I said had the opposite effect and thanks to Richard's determination and perseverance, we started dating in July 2001. The four-year age gap I'd fretted about proved irrelevant and I fell for him hook, line and sinker. It helped that he was the total opposite of my father and that he cared deeply for his own family.

By November we were living together, and by March 2002 he had proposed to me on a cold morning in North Yorkshire, where his parents, Ann and John, live. We'd arrived for the weekend and it was only the second time I'd met his family.

On the Saturday morning, Richard woke me at around eight thirty and, not being a morning person, I wasn't too happy about it. I needed a lie-in in the snug, warm bed where, unlike our London flat, there was no noise at all. But Richard insisted, so eager to please him and his parents, I dragged myself out of bed and had breakfast with them.

Both Ann and John were in their mid-fifties and very active people. Ann is very artistic and John is a retired scientist and a talented musician who plays several instruments and enjoys playing in local bands. Ann agreed to lend Richard her car, and we drove for ten minutes into the middle of nowhere. All I could see was misty moorland.

Taking my hand, Richard walked me through the freezing cold until we came to a big round rock, which he told me is the Great Stone of Fourstones – or the 'Big Stone' as it's known locally. It was left by a glacier straddling the border of North Yorkshire and Lancashire tens of thousands of years ago.

'It's always been a very special place for me. I also spent the arrival of the new millennium here,' he explained.

Seeing it meant a lot to him, I tried to stop myself from shaking with the cold and smiled at him when he suggested we walk up it. Not having been to the toilet since getting up and unable to resist any further, I rather unromantically answered, 'Yes, but I need to pee first! Sorry!'

Walking behind the Big Stone, I did just that, which is no mean feat given the number of layers I was wearing!

We walked up the steps carved into the side of the stone. As I reached the top, dreaming of returning to Ann and John's fireside, I turned to find Richard down on one knee, holding a small box with a ring glittering inside.

'Beatrice, will you marry me?' he asked.

I was stunned into silence. Never in a million years did I imagine this would happen – not to me, not now. I'd expected that we would live together for a long time, but marriage?

Eventually he said, 'I hope it's the cold stopping you from giving me an answer...'

How could I say no? But we'd only been together for eight months! Then I blurted out, 'Yes!'

Slipping the ring, specially made by our dear jeweller friend Ben, onto my finger, he stood up and we held each other. The rest is a bit of a blur, but I do remember returning to the family home and telling his mother.

'Mum, Beatrice has something to say to you,' said Richard, smiling.

Ann looked at my shocked face and thought we'd had a car crash. All I could do was raise my left hand and show her the ring.

Ann's face lit up and she immediately gave me a heartfelt cuddle. Apparently, Richard's proposal plan was a well-kept secret. Nobody knew, apart from Ben.

Ann ran upstairs to tell John the big news straight away and he confirmed that it was an 'excellent idea'. How very English!

Ann then called all her family, who live in Liverpool, to tell them the good news, and I called Zia Mena, who on more than one occasion had said, 'Please get married so I can die in peace.' She cried on the phone and thanked God for answering her prayers. She also said my mother would now rest in peace too.

I'd already taken a quiet moment for myself to tell Mum. It brought tears to my eyes. She would have been so happy to see me settled and marrying into such a lovely family. I'd always thought my mother sent all the important people onto my path to look after me, and now she'd done it again.

Before going to Liverpool to meet Richard's extended family, as we'd already planned, we spent some time in the garden, taking commemorative photos under a blossoming cherry tree. It turned out to be a beautiful crisp winter's day and we look so happy in the photos. Perfect.

On the way to Liverpool, I called my friend Francesca. I owed this day to her, because she'd found me the job that led me to meet Richard. We laughed a lot and immediately started talking about dresses and bridesmaids. It was all so surreal.

Eventually we arrived at the home of Richard's grandparents – Ann's parents, Sheila and Eric. One of Ann's sisters, Lindsay, was there with her family, but her other sister Jane couldn't be there as her husband wasn't well.

I'd never been so nervous. *What would they think of me, a girl from Sicily?*

I'd heard a lot about Sheila and Eric. Richard adored them, like everyone else in the family, and very soon I would discover why. I had the impression that Sheila, or Nanna, was a very strong lady who was still calling the shots – a true matriarch – and I loved that.

Ann had admitted to me that when she'd told Sheila that Richard had a girlfriend from Sicily, she wasn't very impressed. She had very strong opinions about Sicily, like many other people who associate it with the Mafia. I've heard this so many times. Apparently, Eric would have loved to have gone to Sicily but Sheila always refused. Although Sorrento was one of their favourite holiday destinations, that was as far south as she would go.

Ann told me that when she'd shown her a photo of me, after taking in every detail she'd said I looked nice and had good teeth. Well, I guess that's something.

Little wonder I was so nervous. I had to impress someone who already didn't like where I came from. I had to try to change her perception of my culture, and to add to the pressure, Richard was the oldest grandson and the first one to get engaged. It had been a very quick step from girlfriend to fiancée. Under the circumstances, I would be suspicious myself.

When we walked in and I was introduced as Richard's fiancée, I had such a lovely reception. Everyone looked very happy to meet me and congratulated me on the engagement. But I now knew what they'd meant about Sheila. She was a beautiful lady in her eighties, with impeccable hair, make-up and manicured nails. She was smartly dressed and wore perfectly chosen jewellery. Due to an unfortunate accident a few years earlier, she was in a wheelchair, but this didn't take away any of her class and powerful charm. She meant business!

At first, we had a very pleasant exchange, with Sheila asking me questions and listening very carefully to my answers. Slowly,

I began to feel more relaxed, and I felt things were going well. There was a lot to take in. I got on great with Lindsay, and her shy, seven-year-old, blond and blue-eyed daughter Sophia was adorable. I also talked to Ann's other sister Jane on the phone, which was more difficult than being introduced in person, but again, Jane was very welcoming and easy to talk to.

We went out for lunch on Liverpool's historic waterfront, the Royal Albert Dock, where Eric – affectionately called 'Chop' by the family – stole my heart. I never thought that one person could compensate for my own lack of grandparents, but he did. He was the sweetest granddad I could ever imagine, and so much more besides. Chop was the ultimate old-school gentleman, so smart in his three-piece suit with a handkerchief in his jacket pocket. A David Niven lookalike, including an identical pencil-thin moustache, he also had similar mannerisms to the actor. I felt like I was in an old black-and-white movie when he kissed my hand (a tradition he continued every time we met subsequently) and stood up after me whenever I left the table and again when I returned.

Before we left, I overheard Sheila telling Richard, 'You're on to a winner – she's a keeper!' I was absolutely delighted to have passed the test and be welcomed into this wonderful family in such a way.

In the car on the way back to Ann and John's house, I felt overwhelmed with a sense of incredulous happiness and gratitude. This was the family I had dreamed of, and from now on I was a part of it.

Once more, my thoughts turned to my mum. '*Grazie, Mamma*. You did it. You can truly rest in peace now. I'm going to be fine.'

Richard and I deliberated over which month to choose for our wedding day. I'm not sure why, really, as wherever you are in the UK, the chances of rain are high whether it's summer or winter. In the end we plumped for May – the date of the FA Cup final, no less, though we didn't realise this when booking it.

As tradition goes, we should have been married in the bride's native territory and I did think about it, but once I realised how much bureaucracy, travelling and extra expense was involved, I decided against it. Instead, we opted for Cumbria's beautiful Lake District, as it was close to where Richard had been brought up. We chose a beautiful Grade II-listed Victorian mansion near Lake Windermere.

Both Richard and I fell in love with this elegant and evocative building, perched on a hill overlooking Morecambe Bay and the more distant mountains. Nestled in lush gardens and topiary, it was the quintessential English manor. Outside, the building was a jumble of towers, balustrades, gables and lead-lined windows. Inside, the walls were adorned with wood panels, the lounges dotted with grand leather sofas and large, open stone fireplaces. In winter, log fires crackled beneath the low murmur of guests deep in conversation over cups of tea. For me, it was like stepping back in time, and it was the closest to a castle I could get. Getting married in a castle had been a childhood dream of mine. We even found a beautiful medieval castle, but its remote location would have been too difficult for many of the guests to reach.

As with all best-laid plans, there was a hitch and the beginning of the wedding weekend didn't start well at all. On the Friday, Edoardo and his family were due to arrive at London's Stansted Airport, where Richard and I would pick them up, and then we would all drive up north together in a rented car. But just as we were about to leave our flat, Edoardo phoned to say their flight had been cancelled. The airline was trying to put people on different flights but couldn't guarantee anything at that point.

My heart sank. Edoardo was meant to be giving me away, and Atena, who was then four, was one of my three small bridesmaids. They were the only members of my close family attending the wedding and I couldn't believe this was happening. Eventually Edoardo called back to say they were about to be transferred to a different airport, about two hours away and would get on a flight in the afternoon. They were due to arrive in London in the early evening. With the drive up to the Lakes expected to take four or five hours, assuming there were no delays, our estimated arrival time at the hotel was now around midnight.

Although relieved to know they would eventually arrive, I couldn't help but be upset over how the night before my wedding was turning out. All the rest of the family and some friends would be there by afternoon and we were supposed to have dinner together. I was meant to relax with my friend Grazia, who was sharing my room that night, and was looking forward to an early night so I could be blissfully relaxed the morning after.

After picking up Edoardo and his family, we headed straight up north, watching the weather grow worse every mile of the way. It wasn't just rain but a storm with a torrential downpour, and the treacherous conditions meant that we had to drive really slowly. Richard and Edoardo took turns at the wheel and were soon both exhausted. The only one who was oblivious to all of it was Atena, who slept like an angel throughout almost the whole journey. Bless her.

Arriving at the hotel at two in the morning, we were all shattered but relieved to be there. Some friends and family had waited up for us, and after a quick drink, I went to my room, where Grazia was waiting for me.

I promptly burst into tears. She had a bath ready for me, full of bubbles and relaxing oils, but it was clear that I needed more than that to relax and luckily she also had a bottle of champagne on ice. As she covered me with a foul-smelling mud face mask and put two slices of cucumber over my tired eyes, we raised a glass to toast my forthcoming wedding and laughed at the situation.

After a long bath and more glasses of champagne, I was finally relaxed enough to face my Big Day. Imagine! The next day, I, Beatrice Curcurace from Taormina, would become Mrs O'Sullivan!

Once in bed, I turned round to face Grazia and then, looking like I'd just had an epiphany, sat up and whispered, 'Grazia,
do you realise that tomorrow I'm actually getting married?'

Grazia smiled at me and whispered back, 'I do, but I'm not
sure you do! Let's try to sleep now, otherwise no amount of
concealer will cover the dark bags under your eyes, my dearest
bride-to-be.'

I looked at the clock and gulped – I had to get up in four
hours. The rain was still coming down heavily and the strong
winds were crashing against our big windows. I decided to let
it soothe my sleep rather than upset me. I had avoided looking
at the weather forecast for days, as we have a saying in Italy:
'*Sposa bagnata sposa fortunata*', which more or less translates as
'A rain-soaked bride is a lucky bride.' In that case, I was about
to be very lucky indeed.

I closed my eyes and drifted off to sleep.

When the alarm went off, the first thing I did was look out
of the window to discover it was still raining, but I decided it
wasn't important and it wasn't going to spoil the day. From that
moment on, I was extremely grateful to have had Grazia with
me, who arranged my schedule with military precision and even
prevented me from bumping into Richard before the ceremony.
Not that I'm overly superstitious, but you don't really want to
tempt fate on your wedding morning, do you?

One of the funniest, happiest memories I have of that
morning is seeing a man walking through reception, completely
hidden by the huge cardboard box he was carrying. Shouting
and panting, he asked in a very strong Italian accent, 'Excuse
me, where is the wedding?' looking like he was about to drop
the box on the floor and then collapse himself. I then realised
that it was my cousin Stefano, who had come with his family.
Apart from my brother and his family, he was the only one who
made it from Sicily. May is a difficult month for people to take
time off in Taormina – everyone is busy working at the start of
the tourist season. I later learned that the fragile contents of the

box was a stunning lampshade handmade out of very delicate glass pieces that originally belonged to a church window. It had miraculously survived its journey in cars, trains and a plane in one piece.

In contrast to the previous day, everything went smoothly. I had my hair done first thing at the local hairdresser by the lake. Shunning a sophisticated up-do, I went for a more natural wavy look, with delicate pearls holding up a few gently twisted locks at the back. Working with the theme, Grazia applied my make-up very naturally to complement my olive skin tone (I managed to get a tan during my hen party weekend in Barcelona). Finally, she helped me step into my wedding dress and I stared at my reflection in the mirror.

Me in a wedding dress! It really was a sight I thought I would never see. I designed it myself, choosing a simple style with the precious help of my friend Julie, a fashion designer. It was a long sleek dress with a small trail and a bolero jacket buttoned at the back. The jacket was made of a delicate French lace and had sleeves with dramatic fluted cuffs. The silvery-blue colour I'd chosen contrasted perfectly with my rather unusual bridal bouquet, which was dominated by bright yellow sunflowers – a request that caused the florist to look at me in a very strange way.

Sunflowers are my favourite flower, maybe because I associate them with the Sicilian sun. Although they're not the easiest or most delicate flowers to use in a bride's bouquet, together with the dainty little white flowers and gentle leaves cascading downwards, they looked stunning. Even if the sheer weight of it meant I wouldn't be following tradition and throwing the bouquet, in case it caused serious injury!

All dressed up and ready to go, I stood at the top of the wooden staircase leading to the ceremony room, surrounded by my bridesmaids dressed in cute pale-blue chiffon dresses and holding single sunflowers. Yet there was one thought on my mind: *Where on earth is Edoardo?* My brother was nowhere to be seen.

Just before I seriously started panicking, he appeared, still arranging his tie and walking in a typical Italian 'What's the rush?' way. He gazed at me and I swore I could see tears in his eyes.

'You look beautiful,' he said. Apparently, he and his family had taken the opportunity to go for a boat trip on Lake Windermere and came back late. As you do on your only sister's wedding day!

Walking arm in arm into the ceremony room, I felt my knees wobble. I'd been far too calm up until now, with no nerves at all, and thus far it had been a lovely, relaxing, joyful day.

As we were about to turn the corner into the room, Stefano came running towards us to give Edoardo his buttonhole flower and looked at me with a huge grin that said so much more than words. I heard the music Richard had chosen: 'Recuerdos de la Alhambra', a Spanish guitar piece by Francisco Tárrega. It's very special for him, as his granddad used to play it, and now it's just as special to me.

The moment I entered the ceremony room and saw all the faces turning to look at me, I felt an overwhelming wave of emotion sweep over me. All these people gathered here from all over the world. Not just Italy and England, but also France, Spain, Belgium, New Zealand and Australia. Dear friends and family, all here to celebrate this special day, when a whole new exciting chapter of our life together was about to start. Hopefully it would prove to be the 'happy ever after' I'd always dreamed of. I was filled with pure joy and happiness, but at the same time there was another thought fighting to come to the fore. It was a deep feeling of profound sadness that my beloved mother wasn't there with me to witness my happiness. I missed her presence so very much.

Somehow, I managed to pull myself back into the moment and realised I had tears streaming down my face. Even more appeared when I reached Richard. Patiently standing waiting for me, he took my hands, and his face beamed with love. For the duration of the service, I barely stopped crying with the emotion of it all.

Just when I finally managed to control my tears, I accidentally looked towards Richard's parents and saw his father John crying. And that set me off again. Thankfully, I was able to pull myself together as our friends Francesca and Heddou delivered their readings, and then Grazia appeared from nowhere to correct my tear-stained make-up. Later, several people told me how emotional and beautiful it was and how they'd shed a tear along with me. Reassuring as it was, I was still embarrassed.

Once the service was finished, I felt a huge sense of relief. Especially after managing to say the word 'solemnly' without stumbling during my vows, something which I'd been worrying about for days. I challenge any Italian to say it correctly. Finally I could stop crying and start enjoying every single moment that was left of the day. We were now firmly Mr and Mrs O'Sullivan – I'd already decided to change my surname after fifteen years of spelling Curcurace a million times to confused English people. Beatrice O'Sullivan – it had a nice ring to it.

Unfortunately, the weather didn't improve, which meant that all the photos had to be taken inside, which was fine, except we had to go in search of the guests who'd slipped off to watch the football match.

The rest of the day went without a hitch and everything was perfect.

Richard gave half his speech in English and half in Italian, which pleasantly surprised so many people. This is Richard all over though. Ever since we started going out, he'd been learning Italian, determined as ever to do the right thing. The best man Anthony's speech makes everyone laugh so much, especially when he showed a poster with a photo of Richard young with long permed hair and praised him for his new fashion style since meeting me. Aida stepped into the father-of-the-bride's shoes and gave a speech that was sweet, funny and emotional all at the same time. Then it was my brother's turn to deliver his short, impromptu speech, which brought the house down. What a wonderful day!

Immediately afterwards, we cuddled and I cried again. Although Edoardo and I weren't brought up with much emphasis on sharing feelings, that was a very special moment I will never forget. Richard and Edoardo also shared a hug.

The evening reception was so much fun. Everything was planned our own way, which was a very good Anglo-Italian mix and we didn't follow many traditions – including the wedding cake, which was a two-tier chocolate cake with two sheep on top. My original idea was to have a cake baked in a volcano shape with two sheep climbing it to represent Sicily's Mount Etna and Yorkshire. But the horrified face of the baker in my parents-in-law's village forced me to rethink. Luckily, I still had a bit of Sicily on the cake stand, as Aida brought le paste di mandorla, traditional almond pastries.

My first dance with Richard was hijacked by a friend who decided to pick up the microphone and sing a song by Ronan Keating instead. Slightly confused but amused, Richard and I sort of danced along with it together. We had two bands playing and both had my now father-in-law John performing in them. People told me they thought he was the coolest father-in-law ever, and I agreed.

John also had a surprise in store for me. I couldn't believe it when I heard his mandolin playing the upbeat notes of the Tarantella. According to legend, the name of this dance originates from the town of Taranto in southern Italy, where if you were bitten by the poisonous tarantula spider, you would be affected by a hysterical condition known as 'tarantism' and frenzied dancing was the only cure. Apparently, as a ritual, tarantism has roots in the ancient Greek myths. It might sound a bit morbid, but it is in fact a very cheerful and playful dance.

I loved how everyone stood up to dance, even though almost no one knew how to dance the tarantella or indeed what it was. A fusion of two cultures inspired by a spider bite. Perfect.

The rest of the evening was split between an Italian playlist, where all the Italians danced and sang together while everyone else watched on amused, and a DJ playlist Richard put together, including some of his own music. There was something for everybody. It was great to see people having so much fun together but also to see our friends and family, who had never met before, mingling and getting on so well.

I stopped for a second and tried to take everything in. All of a sudden, I realised that this moment, this here and now, was never going to happen again. The people most dear to Richard and me were all in one place at the same time, celebrating our union. Our future. Our life together. In that single moment, I had the certainty that my life had finally turned the most important corner. Marrying Richard was the best thing that could ever have happened to me. That day, the O'Sullivans and Curcuraces became one family.

Even if we never manage to extend it with a family of our own, as we'd both love, there's a lot to be grateful for, I concluded. *Dare we even dream of more?* At that point, no.

19

Realisation Day

I'd been perched on the toilet with my eyes closed for five minutes, praying hard. With bated breath, I opened my eyes, stared at the little window of the white plastic stick in my hand and saw it was showing a line. A very definite, strong blue line. I was pregnant! For a second time! Leaping up, I shouted downstairs to Richard, who was working from his home office.

Once we'd decided to leave London, he took the chance to really test his talents and do something he'd always wanted to do: set up his own research company specialising in the music industry. I'd already been made redundant but as I'd got a laptop and a lovely husband out of my job, I wasn't too upset. My new role would be working with Richard as a researcher, which meant that if we were lucky enough to ever be blessed with a family of our own, I could combine the role with being a hands-on mum. So when Erica came along in August 2004, only fifteen months after our wedding, despite all my worries about my age affecting my fertility, we became a bit giddy. We dared to start to wonder if we could add another baby to our family. And here, in this bit of plastic, was proof that we could.

Richard was as delighted as I was, and we revelled in our good fortune with a big hug in the hall for a few moments before he raced back into his office to take an important call from a client in America. I peered in at Erica and marvelled at her sheer perfection, wondering who would be next in the nursery. A sudden wave of nausea and exhaustion swept over me, and I took it as a good sign. I'd had a very easy pregnancy with Erica and really had been blooming, as everyone kept telling me, but this one felt very different already.

Falling back into bed, I managed a catnap, until Erica woke me and I started the ritual of a toddler's breakfast before dropping her off at my mother-in-law's house so I could concentrate on my work. Thank goodness for my husband's supportive family.

Although I never harboured any real hope that my father would have any sort of traditional loving relationship with my children – his grandchildren – by then there was no chance of it at all. Six weeks earlier – and less than a year since our all-important family visit – I received the news that he'd passed away and we found ourselves flying back for the funeral, which was all just a blur. Perhaps I'd blotted it out, filed it all away for processing at a later date, when my mind and my time would be less preoccupied with babies and work. When I would be ready to cope with the strange mix of emotions of it all.

Back home, I settled down and tried to concentrate on the research tasks facing me. All morning though, something was niggling me. The seed of doubt first sown by Richard in Taormina was taking root with the new knowledge that I was expecting another child. I needed to know more about my own family's peculiar history. Yet at the same time, for some reason I felt anxious about what I might discover.

It took another couple of hours of mulling over all sorts of past stuff before I finally bit the bullet, poured myself a coffee from my Italian *caffettiera* and sat down in a living-room armchair with my laptop. My Italian coffee is a tradition that's important to me. Not because I can't drink instant coffee, like the many Italians who indignantly insist that it's not proper coffee, but because I love the aroma that immediately permeates my house, infusing my English home with the essence of Italy.

As I googled 'Edoardo or Edward Cecil Page, Sicily' I expected very little to come up, but instead the screen filled with results. Something with this name and the name D.H. Lawrence caught my attention. I soon realised that it was in actual fact a letter written by *the* D.H. Lawrence and addressed to *the* Edward Cecil Page. It was dated 30 March 1922 and sent from the island of Ceylon, now Sri Lanka but then a British colony.

I shouted Richard's name and he came running from his study, thinking something serious had happened.

'Look at this!' I said with a huge grin on my face.

Richard was as keen to discover the truth about my family's past as I was – perhaps more so, as he didn't share my apprehension about what it might unearth – and peered eagerly over my shoulder at the screen.

The letter specifically mentioned Taormina, and Edward was described in the footnotes as 'an Englishman who has resided in Sicily since before 1914; a man of some wealth and an intimate friend of the Duca di Bronte, he lived in a large house on the hills above Spisone beach'. Spisone beach was where I went every summer with my mother, and I still visit now whenever I return. So there was no doubt whatsoever that this was my Signor Edoardo.

We scrolled down and continued to find letters and extracts from books and journals. Then in one of these links we came across the name of Teddy Cecil Page.

I made a new search with 'Teddy', and more links came up with more references to him. We soon realised that Teddy was what his American friends called him. To our amusement, we discovered that an American author called David Macan even wrote a fictional book based on him called *The Duke of Forza d'Agro*, published in 1951. This was where we started to find out more about who this person – so important in my family's past yet so unknown to me – really was. The more revelations we discovered about his exciting social life, the more everything seemed to fall into place.

We also began to learn about the darker, seedier side of his life, though it quickly became apparent that this wasn't so much the 'hidden side' of Cecil Page; it was in fact a part of his public persona that everyone knew about but chose to turn a blind eye to.

The more we read, the more we realised that Teddy Cecil Page's bohemian lifestyle wasn't only the talk of the town but renowned throughout all the exclusive social circles of his day. The flawless image of the respectable Englishman I'd grown up with started to darken before my eyes. Was this really the same saint-like gentleman who'd rescued my father from a life of poverty and saved my mother from dying of typhoid? The one who'd paid for their wedding and their lavish homes and lifestyles? The man that everyone in Taormina had spoken of with such deference and respect?

The words scrolled past on the screen, but I struggled to comprehend the magnitude of the character transformation that was happening in front of me. This cultured old bachelor, who'd been a constant reference point in my life story, was now becoming something altogether different. The quaint eccentricities that I'd heard of so many times and so readily accepted without question now didn't seem quite so charming. And the concept of an old unmarried man taking a young boy into his home to live with him didn't feel quite so normal anymore.

I looked up at Richard for confirmation that I was reading this right, and his jaw dropped as much as mine.

'Keep going,' he said, shrugging and simultaneously shaking his head.

My fingers trembled and then one quote made me catch my breath, practically knocking the air out of my lungs:

Teddy Cecil Page was extremely wealthy and owned a palace in Taormina that bestowed upon its owner the title of Duke. Teddy was biding his time at Shepherds Hotel until the authorities allowed him to return to Sicily. Before the war, visitors to the palace were sometimes surprised to find that the entire palace staff, the head butler included, were all under the age of thirteen. At the first sign of puberty, they were relieved of their duties and retired on a small pension. The locals thought this slightly eccentric, but as their teenage children were all bringing home pensions, it was not to be sniffed at.

Then another even more shocking quote:

Teddy Cecil Page has been miserable all year, due to two things: 1) a really horrible American called Steve Cain stole his little boyfriend Ciccio and thus divided the whole town into an absolute war: those for Teddy, and those for Cain – Cain is very rich and bought a villa here; 2) he is the 'hero' of David Macan's novel *The Duke of Forza D'Agro* and Teddy feels very betrayed by Macan. Actually, it is a bad and silly book, only worth reading because of one terribly funny scene.

Ciccio... my father.

As if in some strange nightmare, I kept searching – 'Cain... Page... Taormina' – and a quote from a Truman Capote biography came up:

For months the patrons of the Americana were captivated by the continuing soap opera of Teddy Cecil Page, a moneyed Englishman and a decades-long resident of Taormina who sometimes stopped by to see Truman and Jack on his way to his own house in the hills.

'He liked beautiful boys, and he turned them into very good and accomplished servants,' said Truman. 'When he was ready for a new one, the hill families around Taormina would vie for him to consider their sons for adoption. Then a rich American came to town, bought a big house, put in a swimming pool and drove around in a large car. At the time Teddy had a boy of thirteen, Ciccio, who was the greatest love of all the boys he had ever had. The American spied him and stole him away – the kid was just undone by the swimming pool and the car. After that, it was open warfare in that town! People were outraged that the boy had gone off and left Teddy, and they tried all kinds of voodoo to kill off the American. But none of it worked. The boy stayed with him and was eventually married in his house.'

Obviously the end wasn't quite accurate, as we knew that Ciccio did go back to Edward and celebrated his marriage to my mother at Edward's house. But there was no doubt that my father loved cars. He was the first person in Sicily to own a Ferrari, as documented in an old and faded newspaper article still framed and proudly on show in the kitchen at Villa Sole.

I was utterly speechless. How could I not have seen this? How could I have been so blind? So naive?

Richard squeezed my hand and asked if I was OK. The truth is that I really didn't know. It was all happening so quickly, and it was an awful lot of complicated information to process, on top of my father's death. I was completely blindsided by it all. I appeared to have turned a key that unlocked a huge family secret and I had no idea how I was going to deal with it. If it was all true, it would explain so many of the problems of my past and shed an entirely new light on everything I'd been told and so readily taken at face value.

What would I do now and where would I go from there?

For now, if I listened to my instincts, probably nothing and nowhere. I needed to think and look after this little baby growing inside me.

20

Joining the Dots

Signor Carlo La Floresta
(Elderly neighbour of the Curcurace family, Taormina, writing
in 2010)

Dear Beatrice, my fellow villager,

Sorry if I did not reply sooner but I had to search deep into my memories, as more than eighty years have passed. I knew every single member of your family, both on your mother Linetta's side and on your father Ciccio's side. When I was twelve years old I had a job as a waiter in the local bar Garufi, where I worked long hours for very little pay. The bar was in an alley, which led to another small alley where your mother lived with her family. I remember your grandfather Beppe was wearing an eye patch (he lost his sight in Russia during the First World War).

I knew your father's family even better. At the beginning of the forties they lived in Via Paterno and then in Via Cuseni, where I also lived. I am sorry to have to tell you the sad, harsh truth but those were very poor times. Your *nonni* [grandparents], *zie e zii* [aunts and uncles] – ten of them – lived all together in a shabby room. In that house, like many others in Taormina, there was no electricity, water or even a toilet! I clearly remember your grandmother, but not your grandfather. And I distinctively remember your great-grandmother, Gina Lorenza. She used to sell *ficalinni* [prickly pears] on the road to earn *poche lire* [a little money].

Your father was not part of my group of friends, as he was younger than us, but I was a good friend of your uncle Alberto. Alberto was very small and thin with a delicate constitution, so while in *scuola elementare* [primary school] we gave him the nickname 'Schiggitta', which refers to something small, almost skeletal and a bit ugly. The nickname was then passed on to your father.

What I can tell you about your father is that, more or less as a child, he was helping a neighbour, Donna Sarafina Ragusa, who had a stable with goats and cows. Normally, he would get food to bring back home as a reward, as she also had a vegetable plot in her estate.

From then on, my memory fades a little as I am now ninety-five. I do remember that after that your father and his family had to change house and went to live near Signor Edoardo. It was Rosario Privitera, employed in Villa Sole as Signor Edoardo's right-hand man, who introduced your father to Signor Edoardo and got him the job as errand boy, doing little jobs in the house and around the village – or so he said. He must have been ten or eleven years of age.

The boy was made very welcome and worked really hard to be able to bring back food or money to his family.

Due to Rosario Privitera's love of gambling and probably lack of business sense, Signor Edoardo lost one of his properties, Mufabbi. After that, Privitera lost his job, ending up as a taxi driver, and your father took his place. The rest is history.

In Taormina, nobody thought badly of Signor Edoardo's homosexuality. On the contrary, we all envied the people who found jobs in those foreigners' houses – they and their families were sorted for life. Even when they left their jobs, their families would receive a pension. I know dozens of people who worked for those people and they swear they have never been molested. Apparently, there was a silent rule: never molest an employee. Other than that, I don't remember much more except that none of your family studied further than in primary school and one of your uncles worked in the post office. Sorry I cannot recall more but I hope this is of help to you in your research. Remember that they were different days back then. *In bocca al lupo*, Beatrice! Good luck!

I hope your search will be fruitful and never forget your beautiful Taormina.

Carlo La Floresta

21
Seeing the Full Picture

It was a Monday morning, and I was about to head out on the school run. Once again, it was raining heavily and hadn't stopped doing so for days. More than five years had passed since I'd first had the startling realisation about my father's past and his connection with Edward Cecil Page. In truth, it provoked a bit of an emotional breakdown and I had to step away from the whole issue. I had a lot on my plate as it was, with a lively toddler to look after and being pregnant with her brother Oliver.

I was by then the proud parent of a son as well as a daughter – a 'perfect pair'. The family I'd almost never dared dream of was now a reality. Richard worked hard and travelled for his business, so much of the day-to-day childcare was down to me, alongside my role as his researcher. It made for a hectic life, and little energy left at the end of the day to deal with non-essential issues. Well, in any case, that was my reasoning for stepping away from the emotional rabbit hole I'd stumbled across.

It was too much, too soon. A shock to the system that I was glad to compartmentalise. A therapist would no doubt say that I was 'in denial'. Gradually though, the questions I strove to keep tucked away rose to the forefront of my mind. It was usually when I looked at my children, particularly Oliver – so dark and with Italian good looks – and they reminded me a little of my father. I couldn't help wondering how I would feel as Oliver's mother, if I was letting him enter such a strange household as my father had done, so many years before.

So when I woke up that morning to see an Italian-postmarked envelope on the mat, I decided to tell Richard about my intention to pick up from where I'd left off and start the search again. I'd already begun by writing to our family's old neighbour, Signor Carlo, and he'd recently replied to me by post. Everyone else I corresponded with in Sicily would reply by email.

What I didn't know, as I waved the unopened envelope at Richard, was that during these past five years, Richard had secretly continued with his own research into Edward Cecil Page, as he was so fascinated by it that he wanted to know more. Seeing the effect those initial revelations were having on me, he'd made the decision not to tell me about any of it and instead wait for me to show an interest in it all again. And as soon as I did, he produced a folder, which he said contained a dossier of vital information that he'd compiled for me.

He explained that alongside the internet findings, he'd added all the information about Taormina that I'd accumulated over the years through conversations, newspaper articles and any other snippets about my family's past life. Knowing Richard's love of history and research, it shouldn't have surprised me in the slightest. Nevertheless, I was overwhelmed by his thoughtfulness, and though a little fearful, I was immediately intrigued to know what else might be revealed. Placing the folder on the hall table alongside Signor Carlo's unread letter as I ushered Erica and Oliver out of the house, I promised myself that I'd read them both as soon as I returned.

The drive took me through beautiful Lancashire countryside and the picturesque village of Whalley, and with the rain by then having stopped, the bright sunshine dazzled me as it glistened on the wet grass in the fields. All around me, everything was a vivid, deep green, interrupted only by white clusters of poor, sodden sheep. I was so struck by its beauty that I really could almost forgive the relentless depressing downpours of the previous week.

Back home, I sat down with a cup of coffee to read Richard's research and Signor Carlo's letter. Signor Carlo's revelations didn't quite tie in with the seedier impression given by my previous internet research, nor indeed Richard's.

The picture that emerged from Richard's investigations was of the archetypal English gentleman abroad. According to Richard's findings, Edward Cecil Page was a minor member of the English aristocracy, born in 1889 into a genteel life of wealth and comfort. In his later years, he was described as 'a short, dapper man with white hair and a neat little moustache, wearing his usual ensemble of baby-blue shirt, shorts held up by a thick, intricately woven Turkish leather belt and calf-length socks. Around his neck, he wore several gold chains.'

His father, Albert Cecil Page, had made his money in ceramics as chairman of the family business, and by the time Edward was born, the family home was an impressive four-storey property in Kensington, London, staffed by six servants. However, for all this affluence, Albert lived in the shadow of his father-in-law, Vice Admiral Charles Howard, whose daughter Beatrix he'd married in 1876 – the very woman whose name I now bear almost a century and a half later.

Vice Admiral Howard's superior eleven-bedroom Knightsbridge house boasted twelve servants, and it's not difficult to imagine Albert's nagging inferiority complex surfacing whenever he visited his father-in-law. The Vice Admiral had enjoyed a decorated career in the Royal Navy, despite blotting his copybook when a ship sank under his command off the coast of Argentina. Coming from a very distinguished line of military top brass must have helped, and he enjoyed the wealth and influence that flowed through the Howard family right up to his death, three years before his grandson Edward was born.

In his continual quest to move out of his father-in-law's long shadow, Albert moved out of his house and Edward grew up in the salubrious surroundings of a bigger, better family home in Chelsea. This new family abode boasted five storeys and seven servants; still not quite in Vice Admiral Howard's league, but more than enough to ensure that Edward enjoyed a very comfortable upbringing.

By his mid-twenties, Edward had established himself in London's most chic social circles as 'musical', despite being accused of playing the piano with 'rippling inaccuracy'. In those days, being 'musical' was also a euphemism for being homosexual. He'd published songs and waltzes, one of which became a popular hit in London's ballrooms, and it was about this time that he helped fund the education of the young Noël Coward, who was already making waves among London's social elite.

It was also at this time that Edward's father resigned from the family business and Edward found responsibility thrust upon him when he was appointed a director of the company. War broke out two years later, and by 1915 he had signed up to fight, becoming a lieutenant in the Coldstream Guards and serving with distinction in the trenches of Flanders. He was remembered for being extremely brave but always going into battle with a rug, gold pill box and silver flask, and mixing with officers who were also suspected of being 'musical'.

His neat moustache gave him the look of being rather 'spinsterish' and he dressed in a pristine manner, with his shorts and shirt ironed with a side (as opposed to front) crease. In restaurants he was equally fussy if the table wasn't set quite to his liking. But he was also renowned for his wit, kindness, supportiveness and discretion during his seven years of service. (This was at least heartening reading, as it gave me hope that, if nothing else, he was kind to my young father.)

At the age of forty, he retired from the family business, finally severing all Page family ties to it that his father had established seventy years earlier. But by this time, Edward had already extended his horizons far beyond London, to Taormina, where he would spend much of the remainder of his life and where he would go on to play such a major role in the life of my father and, indirectly, my life also. What started off as a winter holiday destination eventually became his home, and Taormina is where he chose to be buried – coincidentally or not, opposite my maternal grandparents' grave.

Today, Taormina is a summer destination, but between the end of the nineteenth century and the early decades of the twentieth, it was in winter that a bohemian elite of artists and intellectuals from northern countries would gather there to spend the cold season in such a beautiful climate and dramatic scenery. The list is long and impressive: Goethe, Dumas, Brahms, Klimt, Wagner, John Steinbeck and Oscar Wilde, to name but a few.

Back then, Continental European travel was the rare domain of the wealthy and the adventurous, and Edward Page entertained a fascinating mix of socialites, bohemians and authors. These ranged from his friend, the Prince of Wales and future king Edward VIII, who may even have visited Villa Sole, to authors Rupert Nichol-James and Truman Capote. He also maintained a regular correspondence with D.H. Lawrence. Edward became particularly close to Nichol-James.

Twenty years his junior, Nichol-James was the son of one of his fellow Coldstream Guards officers, and in 1930 the two of them embarked on an exotic tour. Sailing from Syracuse, an ancient town a little down the coast from Taormina, to Alexandria, the pair spent time in Cairo before travelling through Palestine, Lebanon, up to Cyprus, then Athens. They journeyed up to Vienna and finished in Bavaria. The two got on well enough on their travels to embark on further joint voyages to South America and Central Africa.

Edward had started visiting Taormina sometime in the 1920s, purportedly for health reasons, though also because he enjoyed the growing crowd of northern European bohemian misfits. His English money went far in inter-war Sicily and he bought large tracts of land in the twenties and thirties, building the town's youth centre – and of course my childhood home.

He built Villa Sole as an eccentric mix of his old English world and the Mediterranean one. A quintessentially English library gives way to a lemon-tree-lined terrace and terracotta roofing, while dark, stately-home corridors open to sun-soaked balconies decorated with stucco sculpture and gently screened by traditionally green blinds. Among its many treasures, the library even houses an 1896–99 collection of the American edition of *The Yellow Book* with illustrations by Aubrey Beardsley – something that would look at home in a museum.

In many ways, Edward built Villa Sole in his own image: a curious blend of England and Sicily, never quite one or the other. Original portraits by the German photographer von Gloeden – one of which initially sparked my research – greet visitors from the walls of the main living room. Erotic drawings decorate the ornate bathrooms. His subjects, young Sicilian boys, were nicknamed '*chiddi d'a tila*' – those of the cloth – by the locals. Some people think the term refers to the extravagant outfits the boys wore – pieces of cloth wrapped around them and wreaths adorning their heads, like Greek gods. It was a term they also used to describe the English and German homosexual men who visited the town. In fact, the locals perceived these particular tourists as spiders spinning webs to catch the innocent, naive boys, which they would then devour. In this case '*tila*' means web.

If you add to this decadent ambience a spellbinding 'sun-stroke' feeling that never seems to leave you in the summer, it's an odd combination of art, culture, history and seediness. Edward probably ended up in Taormina for a number of reasons. His experiences in the killing fields of Flanders seem to have broken both his mind and body, so the attraction of a warm, dry climate for restorative purposes would have been clear. But there's also little doubt that he could more comfortably be himself in Taormina, a place where the locals were willing to turn a blind eye – *omertà* – to his homosexuality, which, outside the relatively small bohemian circles, Edward had to keep hidden back in London, as homosexuality was still illegal in the UK.

In Taormina, though, things were very different. Although early twentieth-century Sicily was more conservative than the UK, the poverty of the Sicilians meant they were willing to bend their principles for the money-making opportunities offered by the growing number of rich bohemian visitors. But this financially motivated tolerance enabled the emergence of something much more sinister.

Taormina's bohemian playground reputation started to attract seedy but wealthy visitors – women as well as men – who could indulge appetites that wouldn't be tolerated at home. These 'Barons', as they were known, would arrive on *Il Treno dei Baroni*, the specially charted Barons' Train. The London–Paris– Taormina train would stop in Rome, where an extra carriage arriving from Berlin would be attached. Its sleeper carriages would bring more lusty European paedophiles into town to buy the easily available services of its poor young boys. Tragically, one of them could have been my father. It was a staggering revelation, but by this stage I was in a different frame of mind from when I'd started my journey of discovery. By then, I was able to deal with it, to process and comprehend the incomprehensible.

22

Emily

'You're not going to believe this!'

I looked up from helping Erica with her homework, a little bit startled at Richard's dramatic entrance. 'What am I not going to believe?' I asked.

'So, I found a couple of online forums where people research family trees and I posted requests for any information about Edward Cecil Page. A few months went by and I'd almost forgotten about them when I received an email from a certain Emily Page...'

Richard let the words settle in. I felt a wave of nervous excitement wash over me as he continued.

'She's Edward Cecil Page's niece! To cut a long story short, her nephew had seen the post, told me about it and gave her my email address. We've spent the last week emailing back and forth, with me explaining who you were, who your father was. It turns out she even met him and your mother!'

I sat back in my chair, not quite able to process the news.

'What is it, Mum?' Erica was trying to keep up with our conversation but was clearly very confused. I reassured her it was nothing and left her to finish her schoolwork on her own while I went to Richard's home office to see what he'd found. Richard sat me down at his desk with his laptop open in front of him, and explained what I was looking at.

'Emily explained to me that Edward Ceil Page isn't spoken about in their family. He was something of a black sheep, and she seems to be the only family member that actually likes to talk about him. She confirmed many of the things we knew and was really interested to hear your family's side of the story, but when I mentioned your father, she told me she had something special to share. That was a few days ago. Then this email arrived.'

I sat forward in the chair and started to read.

Dear Richard,

When I saw you write about Ciccio in your last email it brought back a flood of memories for me. I travelled to Sicily many years ago and met your father-in-law. In fact I went there to meet him. It was a trip that left a big impression on me and I wrote a travel diary which thankfully I still have to this day, even if it is a bit dusty and faded now. What follows is my account of that trip as I remember it from those diaries.

Sicily, June 1960

As the train pulled into the station, smoke from its engine flooded the platform, momentarily immersing the awaiting people. I jumped from my seat, eager to finally set foot on Sicilian soil.

The past week had been one that I would never forget, as the train weaved its way across Europe and these last two days through Italy. Italy's beauty had exceeded my already high expectations. Though of course I had seen Italy in books and on TV, I had not appreciated quite how different it was from England, at least when I got the chance to escape from London to see it.

Everything was different there. The colours were more vibrant, especially the sky, which was a deep and vivid blue that I had never seen in England. Instead of green fields and hedges dotted with cows and sheep, the hills here were filled with olive groves and vineyards. Rather than simply a different country, Sicily resembled a new world, one that I already longed to explore.

Rupert threw down my case from the rack above our heads, pulling out a handkerchief from the breast pocket of his jacket to wipe the sweat that was pouring from his forehead.

'Damn this infernal heat. Let us just get out of this filthy carriage. If this is what passes for first class in this land, I hate to think what the other carriages are like.'

I resisted the urge to smile at my brother's discomfort and instead picked up my case and stepped out onto the platform.

'Signor and Signora Page?'

I turned to see where the voice had come from but before I could respond to the smartly dress hotel porter, Rupert snapped back at him.

'Yes, man, that's us. Now grab our bags and get us out of this hellhole.'

I felt an urge to apologise for Rupert's rudeness.

Whether it was because he spoke no English and had not understood a word that Rupert had said, or whether it was because he was irritated by this haughty Englishman, the porter said nothing as he took our cases and led us to the waiting car.

As the car drove up the road that snaked its way up from the seaside station to Taormina, I gazed down at the sea glistening in the sun, not even hearing the irritated words pouring from Rupert's mouth. I found myself captivated by the sea throughout the train's journey from the port of Messina through to Taormina's station, the track hugging the coast, often so close to the sea that I felt I could reach out and touch it.

We were staying in the Grand Hotel Timeo, which was the best Taormina had to offer – not that you would have thought it based on Rupert's reaction. Nothing in Sicily was going to be good enough for him.

'The sooner we can get our job done and get out of this place the better.' Rupert picked at his food, clearly disliking the hotel's cuisine as much as he did the country.

For my part, I was enjoying every mouthful of food, the likes of which I had never tasted before.

He pushed his plate away with clear disdain, before adding, 'Even this shabby hotel makes me itch.'

'Rupert, you really need to calm down and try to make the most of this trip. And this hotel is wonderful – have you not read the notice in the reception? This place is hundreds of years old and has entertained many famous guests such Kaiser Wilhelm II and King Edward VIII and that D.H. Lawrence wrote *Lady Chatterley's Lover* here.'

'Fantastic, so we're sharing a hotel with a Hun, a king who couldn't keep his pants on and a perverted writer.'

'Surely even you though, Rupert, cannot deny that the view of the sea from the terrace is to die for?'

'It's sea, Emily, just a bloody great mass of water – that is all. You would do well to stop getting distracted by all of this and focus on getting Uncle Edward's money back from that awful little Sicilian man. I'll be damned if I am going to leave here with that filthy peasant having his finger on even a penny of Uncle Edward's money.'

Next day, we sat in the hotel library waiting for our meeting with Francesco Curcurace. It was midday and the heat was stifling even for me. Poor Rupert was sweating right through his three-piece suit. More fool him for overdressing and ordering a pot of steaming hot tea while I indulged in an ice-cold glass of *vino alla mandorla* – almond wine. I for one was going to sample all of the local cuisine I could while I was in Sicily.

'Damn it – he is half an hour late. I said half past eleven on the dot. That's the problem with these damn Italians – no sense of time or punctuality.'

I let Rupert's frustrated words float by my ears as I set my gaze on the glistening sea outside the window. I sometimes wondered whether Rupert and I were born of the same stock, as at times he seemed to be everything I was not. Or perhaps the truth was that I was everything he and my family were not.

Rupert was the perfect English gentleman – he'd studied at Eton and Oxford, had a successful career in business and was now on a path to Parliament. But I had never felt truly at home in that world. Which is part of why I had volunteered to join Rupert on this trip. I longed for any opportunity to break free of the confines of polite London society, and besides, Uncle Edward intrigued me. I'd never met him – in fact he was rarely spoken of, especially by my father. That is, until he died, at which point the pound signs started flashing in Rupert's eyes.

It transpired that Uncle Edward had lived something of a bohemian life here in Taormina and somehow had fallen in with a young local lad and had left him everything. Rupert and my father were, of course, horrified when the news finally wound its way back to London. To add insult to injury, Uncle Edward had insisted on being buried here. The more my family were angered by the developments, the more I found myself drawn to this unconventional cad.

A knock at the door pulled me from my thoughts. We both turned to see a smartly dressed man, a few years older than me but much younger than Rupert. His sun-kissed skin contrasted our pale faces, and he had a confident bearing as he strolled in. Yet, there was something about his wide and slightly nervous smile that made me wonder whether the confidence was more act than actual. He was accompanied by an older man, also dressed smartly but without the handsome features of the other.

'Mr and Miss Page, welcome to Taormina. I am Francesco Curcurace, but everyone calls me Ciccio.'

He spoke with a very strong accent and had some difficulty saying the words. While I was flattered that he had made the effort, Rupert was not impressed in the slightest.

'Good God, how are we meant to communicate with him – he cannot even speak English.'

Before I had a chance to respond, the other man interjected in English to explain that he was going to translate for us. Rupert insisted on talking straight at this dashing young man as if he understood everything he said and the translator was not even there.

'I do not know who you think you are and what tricks you played to get your dirty hands on my dear uncle's money and property, but it ends now, right here. You will hand over the deeds to his houses, control of his bank accounts and access to all of his shares in Geneva. Do not think for a moment that I am not familiar with every corner of his finances, boy.'

Francesco stared at Rupert as the other man hurriedly translated the words. As each phrase worked its way into Italian, his expression steadily changed from one of genial confidence to nervous anger. He spoke quickly to the translator, not taking his eyes off my brother for even the briefest of moments.

The translator looked sheepishly at Rupert and spoke.

'Mr Curcurace disputes your claims. He says that in all the years in which he was fortunate to enjoy Mr Cecil Page's friendship, he did not once hear your name mentioned, nor did any of your family ever think to visit him. He and his wife were there for Mr Cecil Page right until the end of his life. He was a lonely man who had been abandoned by his family. Yet, now there is money at stake, here you are, running as fast as your legs will carry you.'

Rupert jumped to his feet in a fury. 'How dare you talk to me like that, you insolent little peasant. Do not pretend to know my uncle better than I. I am his blood; you are nothing more than a foreign parasite that has sunk his teeth into a vulnerable old man. You have no right to his assets. That is my inheritance, and you will hand it over to me herewith.'

Once again Francesco listened as the words were translated. He was obviously unsettled by the anger of this man, who carried a clear air of authority, and the confidence he had borne as he entered the room was now entirely gone, but in its place was a steely determination.

I wondered what he must have been thinking at this moment. By all accounts, he had spent most of his life looking after my uncle, and now this angry stranger from England was claiming everything from him and insinuating that he had been anything but sincere in his actions. I could not help but feel sympathy for him in that moment.

He pulled out a document from a bag by his side and spoke quickly in Italian, pointing to the paper. My brother snatched it from him as the translator spoke. As he read, his face reddened with fury.

The translator explained. 'This is the last will and testament of Edward Cecil Page, drawn up five years ago, long before he fell into ill health. As you can see, everything here is in order. All of Mr Cecil Page's assets are listed and bequeathed to my client Francesco Curcurace.'

For once, Rupert was silent. He read and reread the will with disbelieving eyes, shouting, 'Lies, all lies.' But he knew that there was no disputing the will. He stormed over to the other side of the room and stared out of the window for a while, patches of sweat now working their way through the back of his jacket.

Eventually he spun round. 'I do not know what you did to compel my uncle to have this ridiculous document drawn up, and when I am back in England, I will have the finest lawyer money can buy dissemble it. But until then, there is one thing you have forgotten. His shares in Geneva.'

Francesco smiled for the first time since sitting down and, without breaking eye contact, with Rupert, called out in English in his thick Italian accent, 'Mr Gunther, will you please come in.'

Though I knew that the entire purpose of our trip was falling away in front of our very eyes, all I could do was try to imagine how this handsome young man had surrendered his youth to care for my aging uncle.

An impeccably dressed man in his fifties walked into the room with a sheaf of papers in his hand. He bowed his head slightly and spoke to Rupert in perfect English that had only the slightest hint of an accent.

'Mr Page, let me introduce myself. I am Gustav Gunther, representative of the Swiss Free Bank. Your uncle was my personal client for many years and entrusted me with management of his portfolio of shares. Over the years I came to know Mr Cecil Page very well and I would like to think that we developed something of a friendship. He trusted me implicitly and was very clear when he instructed me to transfer ownership of his portfolio to Mr Curcurace in the event of his death. These are copies of the legal documents confirming the transfer, which you are free to take with you for your lawyers to assess. I am confident that you and they will find that everything is in order.'

Rupert snatched them from him without a word. In that moment I knew my brother was finally accepting defeat, even if he would not show it.

After reading the documents, he flung them on the table and stormed out of the room, shouting as he did so, 'Do not think you have won, that your lies and fabrications will fool anyone.'

The room fell silent. After a while I got to my feet, Francesco standing as I did so.

'Mr Curcurace...'

'Ciccio please.'

'Ciccio, please forgive my brother. He sometimes struggles to control his emotions and all of this information has, well, come as a great shock to him.'

I said my goodbyes and left the room, hearing the three men fall into deep conversation as I did so.

Next morning, there was no sign of Rupert so I had breakfast on my own. I had decided to spend the day visiting the ancient Greco-Roman theatre that was literally behind the hotel, but then a waiter brought me a note. To my surprise it was an invitation, addressed solely to me, to visit Villa Sole, signed Ciccio and Linetta Curcurace. The theatre would have to wait for another day.

It took me some time to find the house, and I cursed myself for not having learned any Italian so that I would have been able to ask for directions. When I arrived, the gate was open. I called out but no one answered so I let myself in. I walked down some steps into a courtyard with a mandarin tree in its centre. A woman walked out of the kitchen and I was taken by just how beautiful she was.

'*Benvenuta*, Emily, *benvenuta! Venga!*'

Though she was so friendly that I easily understood that she was welcoming me, I was relieved to see Ciccio walk out with the translator from the meeting the day before. We sat down under the mandarin tree where there was an impressive display of Sicilian pastries and drinks waiting.

'Emily, *questa e' mia moglie* Linetta.' Emily, this is my wife Linetta.

Linetta took my hand into hers and said, '*Molto piacere di conoscerla.*' It is a great pleasure to know you.

We were soon chatting as if we had known each other for years – well as much as one can relying upon a translator. They explained that they thought I would like to see the house where my uncle had spent so much of his life before dying peacefully.

Looking at this beautiful young couple my age that appeared to be so in love with each other, I could not help but feel happy for them. There was something about this enchanting place that caught you unawares, that pulled you into its gentle mysteries.

'Ciccio, Linetta, thank you so much for inviting me into your home. It means so much to me to be able to see where my uncle lived.'

Ciccio cast a cheeky smile and spoke in Italian. I could not help but smile when the other man translated his words – 'I hope your brother was not offended that we did not invite him also.'

After a while they showed me around the house. I found myself having an unusual sensation of being in a foreign place yet in England at the same time. On one side of a room would be the most traditional of English furniture and decor but on the other traditional Sicilian ceramics and fabrics. It even contained a library stocked with English books and an ancient freestanding globe, both of which were identical to those in my father's house. My uncle had built a home that reflected the same fusion of home and away that had come to define his life.

Eventually it came time for me to leave. We embraced affectionately, knowing that we would never see each other again.

Back at the hotel, I sat on my balcony watching the sun sink behind Mount Etna. As the sky darkened, I reflected on the events of the last two days. Though I knew Rupert would be fuming all of the way back to England, I found myself feeling alive in a way that only then did I understand I had never felt in London. It was then that I realised I had to leave London and find my own path outside of the suffocating confines of my family.

Was it coincidence or was it something about Sicily that caused me to follow a similar path to that of my uncle? As I write this now, after all these years, I think it was indeed something about Sicily. That evening I sat for hours watching the majesty of Etna erupting against the dark night sky. For the first time I began to ask questions of myself and what I truly wanted from life. It was then that I understood I didn't want the future that was mapped out for me, to marry well and raise a clutch of little Etonians. I wanted more than that, and indeed I spent much of the rest of my life wandering the world, always looking for the next place and the next people I had not yet seen or met.

So, Richard, this is why I wanted to tell you about my encounter with your wife's mother and father. I owe them an eternal gratitude. Even though we only met for the briefest of whiles, it was an encounter that set the course for the remainder of my life.

Yours
Emily Page

I sat back in Richard's office chair, overwhelmed. Not only had I finally heard something positive about my father, I had been granted a glimpse into his young life that I would otherwise never have seen. I was left wondering how so much could have changed from that moment in time, when my parents were so clearly in love with each other and my father was a young man finding his confidence and his way in life.

Maybe, just maybe, that had been the start of it all. Knowing my father as I did, I could easily imagine that he saw that victory as confirmation of his abilities and started to believe a little too much in himself. Perhaps that was where the arrogance and conceit first took root.

23

Different Days

A s I lay in the bath, I mulled over my recent discoveries without the distraction of work or young children. My mind raced with possibilities, searching for answers. Was my father abused by Edward Cecil Page? And if so, who was in on this sordid secret? Surely his mother, Concetta, wouldn't have willingly allowed him to take the job at Villa Sole if she'd known that this widely revered gentleman was a paedophile? Yet how did she not suspect?

Despite the hot water of the bath, a cold shiver ran through me as I contemplated what it would be like to put Oliver into a situation like that. The abhorrence of the thought sent another down my body.

Then I recalled the way Signor Carlo had ended his letter, with a gentle reminder that those were different days to any that I'd known. As much as I still couldn't comprehend how it happened, if it did happen, then at least I was beginning to appreciate that they were indeed times when things took place that were so far beyond my own experience of life. Sometimes you can't apply today's paradigms to yesterday's events, however shocking, tragic or inhumane those events might appear. It wasn't just Signor Carlo who helped me understand this, but also Richard's adored grandfather Chop, who I'd enjoyed spending time with of late.

Chop's wife Sheila passed away the year after Erica was born, and after decades of silence he'd started to open up to the family about his experiences in the Second World War. After I met Chop for the first time, Richard had told me about him being in the war, although not in very much detail, which surprised me, as I was already aware of how passionate Richard was about history. But for most of his life, Chop hadn't spoken about his wartime experiences. Possibly because once he came back and started a new life with Sheila, who was a nurse during the war and also had her own experiences, they decided to put everything in the past; to look to the future and never talk about what they'd just experienced.

When Chop began to open up about his past in the RAF, it was a privilege to listen to. Bit by bit, in his own humble way, he hesitatingly shared his experiences – a memory here, a photo there. He'd also kept a few possessions, including a pair of old boots and his missions logbook, which left Richard completely gobsmacked, fascinated and hungry for more.

Reading the logbook, we were amazed to discover that in one of his missions, the air commodore who flew his plane was the actress Helena Bonham Carter's grandfather. Well, to be honest, I was probably more amazed than Richard, who was just feeling emotional about holding that little piece of history in his hands. Perhaps because of Richard and his brother Dave's interest and encouragement, Chop kept giving more and more away each time there was the opportunity.

Chop had been a tail gunner in a Lancaster bomber in the air force, a position that had a life expectancy of around six weeks. Sure enough, after around that length of active duty, his plane was shot down over Germany during a night-time bombing raid. He was only twenty-two.

Up until that fateful night, his life in the air force had been one of intense contrast: drinking with his crew members in a local pub one night, then being shot at in the sky by enemy fighters and anti-aircraft guns the next. He showed us a faded black-and-white photograph of him and one of his crew on a motorbike. This was Sandy, his best friend in the crew, who died when their plane was shot down. Clutching the photo, it was clear that the memory was still very painful to Chop as he told us about Sandy and the attack on their plane.

As a tail gunner, young Chop was separated from the rest of the crew, strapped into a hydraulic-powered rotating gun turret, with gaps in his Perspex window letting the freezing cold, high-altitude air blow remorselessly into his face. All that connected Chop to his crew was an intercom as he stared out into the jet black of the night sky, straining to see the first sign of an enemy attack.

As they approached their target, after hours flying through the cold, dark night, German anti-aircraft guns started to fire up at them. The shells exploded all around them, so close that Chop could smell the cordite in the air, the shockwaves rocking the plane like a small boat in a stormy sea. Throughout this though, the aircrew remained calm and focused on their mission. The bomb doors were opening and they were approaching their target.

Through the intercom, Chop could hear the bomb aimer guiding the pilot – 'Left, left, steady, right, steady, left…' – and then suddenly there was a huge impact just behind his gun turret.

The Lancaster had been hit by a German night fighter plane equipped with upward-firing cannon that had ripped into the underneath of the bomber. Chop's gun turret had been pushed sideways, so the exit to the plane was partially blocked. He tried to move it back into position, but the controls didn't work – the hydraulic system had been shot away.

Eventually he managed to scramble out through the part-open doors into the fuselage, where the wireless operator and Sandy were both stationed.

Once inside the fuselage, Chop opened the side escape hatch to be confronted with roaring flames – the starboard-wing fuel tanks had been hit and were on fire. The wireless operator was next to Chop, and Sandy remained facing the tail, his feet apart, bracing himself.

It was then that the German night fighter came back for another attack. It hit home again – and this time the fire went straight up the middle of the fuselage, through the bomb bay, hitting Sandy. He was killed in an instant, directly in front of Chop.

He and the wireless operator both leaped to the exit door, but the other man staggered and fell to the floor, and appeared to be unconscious. Chop hesitated and then decided to push him out of the escape hatch with his parachute on, rather than face certain death in the burning plane. Chop later learned that the wireless operator had woken up mid-fall and had pulled his parachute in time.

That moment of hesitation had saved another man's life but nearly proved fatal for Chop. No sooner had he pushed his fellow crewman out of the escape hatch than the plane suddenly lurched into a nosedive.

As the plane sped downwards in its death spiral, Chop was thrust to the back of the plane by the G-force. Trapped there, racing towards certain death, his mind was in a spin, asking himself why he hadn't taken his chance to save himself.

Then, inexplicably, the plane suddenly banked and Chop was thrown to the floor. This time he didn't hesitate and immediately threw himself out of the plane, his body smacking against the tail fin as he did so. His parachute took him safely to the ground, though once he landed he realised he'd come down in a field of sharpened spikes. Lady Luck had smiled on him twice that night.

Chop spent the next few days on the run, laying low during the day and walking through the night. Eventually the cold and hunger got the better of him, so he handed himself in to an elderly couple in a cottage, and after being held and interrogated by the Gestapo, he was shipped off to a prisoner-of-war camp in the east.

After some time there, the entire camp was forced to march westwards to avoid the oncoming Russian advance. This forced march in 1945 took place during the coldest winter of the twentieth century, with temperatures often dropping to minus twenty. During this intense cold, Chop and his fellow prisoners had to sleep in barns, outhouses and even in the open. They foraged in icy fields for frozen beets, and many lost toes to frostbite. Chop was fortunate in the latter respect, as he'd soaked his boots in a barrel of discarded oil he'd found, thus waterproofing his boots and saving his toes.

The camp they arrived at was in Luckenwalde, outside Berlin. It was a far bigger camp than they'd been in before and was horribly overcrowded, with POWs being brought in from around the Reich.

Eventually the Russians made it that far too. One morning, the prisoners woke up to find that their guards had disappeared in the night. But before the Russians arrived, a jeep of Americans pulled up at the gate and told the camp that trucks were coming to liberate everyone. However, it was the Russians who arrived next.

The first Russians to come were the tank crews, who impressed Chop with their well-kept uniforms, order and discipline. This, though, was in stark contrast to the main Russian army that followed. They resembled a medieval horde, with male and female soldiers on bicycles, carts and ponies. Wild and undisciplined, they were an absolute mob. They had their women with them, and proceeded to loot and destroy the local towns and villages. There seemed to be no discipline whatsoever, and life was very cheap.

Eventually, the Americans arrived in earnest, with seventy trucks carrying troops to evacuate the American and British personnel. Chop and the other prisoners climbed aboard the trucks, ready for home, and tucked in to some American rations which they were given.

But the Russians were having none of it. After a lot of shouting and shots being fired over their heads, the prisoners reluctantly climbed down from the trucks.

A fierce stand-off continued between the Russians and the Americans, so Chop decided to take his chance, and with three other prisoners he made his way through the perimeter fence at the back of the camp and made a run for it.

Chop and his three companions made their way across Germany towards the American lines. During this time, they had numerous adventures, including drinking schnapps with Russian soldiers. One of their new-found Russian friends provided them with bicycles, and they used these to cycle westwards. Along their way they were approached by a terrified young German girl of about seventeen or eighteen. She was fleeing from the east and was terrified of falling into Russian hands. Chop and his companions decided to take her with them, and took it in turns to transport her on the crossbar of their bicycles.

Finally, they made it to the River Elbe, which marked the boundary between the Russians and the Americans. The bridge had been bombed out, and although there were rope ladders across, the Russian guards were preventing anyone from crossing.

Chop and his companions decided to opt for the 'fortune favours the brave' approach. They pushed their way through the crowds, straight past the Russian guards, threw the bikes into the Elbe and began to cross the river over the rope ladders. Nobody protested, and the American First Army was at the other side to welcome them.

The next problem was what to do with the German girl. They told the Americans that she was Dutch, and they arranged for her to go to a transit camp.

After a number of days of American generosity, Chop flew to Brussels and then London, flying over the White Cliffs of Dover. His ordeal was finally over.

It took a few years for Chop to share all the details, and he was clearly spurred on by the interest the family took.

Later, Richard, his brother Dave and his uncle took Chop to Germany on a once-in-a-lifetime trip, retracing his wartime steps.

It was a trip that included meeting people who had seen his plane crash in flames and visiting the remains of the prisoner-of-war camp at Luckenwalde. Decades later, he was able to sit and talk with people who'd once been the enemy, but now they were all simply Europeans, with no division between them.

Chop was invited in for coffee and cake with a German lady who remembered her parents' farmhouse being destroyed on the night of the bombing raid; toasted his good fortune with photo-snapping locals in the pub that still stood where he was marched after being arrested by the forest warden; listened to a war veteran's memory of seeing him being marched past his house by armed Luftwaffe guards on his way to captivity; and paid silent homage to the ten thousand Russian POWs buried at the site of the former Luckenwalde camp. That, perhaps, was the ultimate legacy for Chop and all those who fought in that most traumatic of wars.

As with so many veterans, Chop never sought any recognition for what he did but simply said he'd been doing his duty like anyone else would. He definitely didn't see himself as heroic, but he undoubtedly was our very own hero. Awestruck, we hung on to his every fascinating word of every vivid account he gave us. But hand on heart, however much he brought those experiences to life, standing in his young boots was still unimaginable. Different days indeed. Is that what I need to accept about my father's past and let it go?

Note: Although Eric 'Chop' Evans was never recognised by the British government, in 2016, a year before he passed away, he received the Legion of Honour (*Légion d'honneur*), France's highest distinction awarded in recognition of both military and civil merit.

24

Different Solutions

R ichard's revelations about Edward Cecil Page continued to haunt me, and I found myself rereading them again and again. As much as I would have liked to sweep away all this new information about my father and Cecil Page's relationship, I found that I couldn't. There were just too many unanswered questions, too many loose ends. Was my father in fact a victim of horrendous abuse to be pitied – and not the emotionally abusive, useless husband and father I saw? Could his trauma be the cause of his recklessness and ultimately his downfall?

In an attempt to gather more information, I decided to fly back to Taormina to visit Signor Carlo, leaving the children in the capable hands of Richard and his mother for a few days.

I arrived at Catania Airport, where my old friend Anna was waiting to pick me up and drive me to Zia Mena's house for a couple of days. The old man I'd come to see was expecting me, so after dumping my bag at Mena's, I headed straight for the cafe in the piazza, where we'd arranged to meet.

Although by then into his late nineties, I was pleasantly surprised to find that Signor Carlo was still sharp and active. Indeed, he hadn't changed much since I'd last seen him. He'd spent his entire life in the town and was one of those people who personified the place he lived in. Everyone knew him, and he exuded a passion for Taormina, its people and its culture, shown through his paintings and poetry.

He greeted me warmly and quickly proved to be a treasure trove of insight and information; the sort of stories and experiences you'd never find in official records or a history book. We sat for hours as he patiently answered my questions as much as he was able. But in truth he couldn't answer the big one: did Edward Cecil Page abuse my father?

Instead, he spoke of what life was like back then, when my parents were young, painting a vivid picture of very difficult times. More than just a series of facts and events, his stories brought that time back to life for me. I could smell the scents, hear the sounds, see the old Taormina in front of me through my own eyes. He had such an incredible memory for details and regaled me with tales of his life.

During the Second World War, Signor Carlo had been a young boy, growing up with the world falling apart around him. But in the way that children can normalise the abnormal, he and his friends simply adjusted to deprivations caused by shortages and occupation by the Germans – that is, until the Allies arrived in 1943 and his world was turned upside down.

'At the time I was only thirteen. I remember the hunger, or as we say, *la fame era nera* – hunger was black.'

He smiled and continued.

'Us kids very often went around the countryside, foraging for food, hoping to find wild fruit such as blackberries, prickly pears and figs, or nuts like chestnuts and walnuts, hidden among the leaves. We were looking for whatever the fruit pickers had missed, often more in hope than expectation. Unfortunately, most often someone before us had had the same idea, so we returned home even hungrier than before.

'The boldest of us boys installed ourselves outside the barracks of German soldiers stationed in anti-aircraft posts in the countryside of Donna Carmela. We stood there, hoping for a soldier to throw us some morsel – a stump of old stale bread given out of sympathy or because one of us had done him a small service.

'I remember like it was yesterday the day that it all changed. It was the ninth of July 1943.

'At around midday we witnessed anti-aircraft fire. A British fighter had appeared, undisturbed, over Taormina. It was a scout. Later the same day, we heard that the Allies had landed in Sicily, but at that stage we didn't realise the significance of this solitary plane. It weaved its way through the anti-aircraft shells, escaping to return to its base, but not before it dropped a small bomb that hit the centre of Taormina. It might have just been one bomb, but for the people of Taormina it was an alarm signal. Immediately, many families started heading for the countryside, seeking the hospitality of old peasant friends, staying wherever there was space – stables, caves or outdoors. Fortunately, it was July, so it was very hot.'

He paused for a sip of coffee, and as he did so, I recalled the stories my mother had told me of this time. She too had left Taormina with her family and spent weeks living in a cave when she was just eight years old. She remembered how my grandmother would leave the cave first thing in the morning and come back in the evening with whatever scraps of food she'd managed to get her hands on. During those difficult days, hunger was relentless. It would be a good day if they were fortunate to chew on a few small raw potatoes.

Signor Carlo placed his cup back in its saucer, sighed and then continued.

'Those villagers who had the foresight to leave Taormina straight away were saved from the bombing that came next. This time, not some small raid but a massive bombardment! It started at around four in the afternoon…'

His thoughts seemed to drift and then, chortling, he said, 'And I must tell you how I survived it, because I was lucky three times over!

'I owe my life to three chance events. Firstly, to my dear friend Turi. He was two years older than me and we were inseparable. Later, he became my brother-in-law, since I married his sister.

'Anyway, that day a local lady had commissioned Turi to take a mattress to a place near Madonna della Rocca, high above Taormina. She was one of those many *Taorminesi* that had decided to spend the night in the nearby countryside. Turi asked me to accompany him, tempting me with the prospect of stopping by the blackberry trees on the way. It was the time of year when the fruit was ripe and they hadn't yet been picked. It was going to be a long walk, since the first trees were around Castelmola, the village perched on top of a rocky outcrop, which itself was so high that it peered down on Madonna della Rocca.

'I accepted enthusiastically. I had nothing else to do except stroll around the neighbourhood, and besides, I would have had a good feast of juicy fruits… even if I knew that the tell-tale red colour of the fruit would stain my face, hands and the few rags I was wearing – incriminating me, should we bump into an angry fruit farmer! But there were water tubs and the fountains to wash in before returning home.

'We walked through the streets of Cuseni, and after climbing the steps that led up the steep hill from Via Circonvallazione, Turi put down his burden and we sat down to rest. If it had been any other day, this moment would have become just another faded memory. But this wasn't just any other day. This was the day the bombs dropped.

'I'd wanted to rest further down, after we'd walked up the steps of Via Salita Ermon Filea, but Turi had insisted we walk on the extra few minutes to the top of the hill first. As I was about to find out, that turned out to be my second stroke of luck – but not until I had my third!'

Signor Carlo chuckled again. He knew I was trying to piece together his story. Leaning forward in his chair, he spoke again, this time with a new intensity.

'I owe my life to Turi, to not stopping sooner and to a German soldier. We were leaning against a wall – a wall that was very soon to be nothing more than rubble – when we heard the sound of planes overhead. We didn't pay much attention, as by then it was normal for planes to be passing over Taormina every day, every hour, but we didn't distinguish whether they were Allied, German or Italian. They all looked the same to us! We saw them coming up from the north – a large squadron. Later, we learned that they were American Flying Fortresses, but in that fateful moment we didn't think much of it, leaning against the wall, catching our breath in the dry heat of the afternoon. We simply thought they would head towards Catania like the other times.

'In the meantime, a German soldier came out of the Castelmola Hotel. He stood right in front of us, looking up at the sky. It was in that moment we realised this wasn't going to be just any other day.

'As he squinted against the bright sky, a look of both recognition and horror instantly flashed across his face. His mouth dropped open and he spun on his heels and ran for shelter. Turi and I looked at each other, our eyes wide with nervous excitement. We didn't need to say anything to each other but instead just ran as fast as our little legs would carry us. We headed for the nearby countryside but only had time to turn into the first shortcut that led to Madonna della Rocca when the bombs dropped.

'I threw myself on the ground, and hell began. There is no other way to describe it. At that moment, I thought it was the end, but strangely I wasn't afraid. The naivety of kids… There was a moment's pause, then I heard Turi shouting, "Jump down!"

'Just below us there was a bridge, and with a leap I found myself beneath it, its arches giving us protection. I don't know how many minutes that hell lasted – maybe only seconds – but we only moved when we heard the sound of the planes fade away. Neither of us said anything. We looked around and saw destruction everywhere. A man who had come from the countryside on his donkey and been near us when we rested had perished. If we hadn't seen the German soldier running for his life, we would not have run for ours.'

Signor Carlo stopped, sat back in his chair and nodded to himself before saying, 'At this point, I have to examine the three circumstances that saved my life. Firstly, if Turi had not called me to accompany him in the countryside, I would have stayed in the area of Cuseni to play with other boys – boys who were instantly buried under rubble thrown onto them by bombs aimed at the San Domenico Palace Hotel, where the Allies believed a senior German officer to be based.

'The bombs were far from accurate though. Only one found its target and even then, it only hit the side, where there was an old church that housed the crypts of ancient nobles. Months later, when we were exploring the rubble, we saw scattered skulls and bones from the shattered graves.

'The rest of the bombs hit Cuseni, claiming many victims – including the lady who had given Turi the task of taking the mattress up to Madonna della Rocca. She hadn't got out as quickly as her mattress had and lost an arm, shattered by rubble.

'Secondly, if we had stopped at the steps of Via Ermon Filea, even just for three minutes, we would have been killed. After that short time, those stairs no longer existed, and the houses that flanked them had collapsed, one on top of the other. Several people died, among them a beautiful girl from the Cuscona family. Her name was Lilla.

'Then thirdly, if that German hadn't run for cover, nor would we have. Those are the three strokes of luck that saved me that day. Without them, I wouldn't be here talking to you now.'

While stirring his coffee slowly and deliberately, Signor Carlo cast his gaze over to the bustling crowds of people in the piazza. I tried to imagine how it must have looked then – how different it must have been to the scene in front of me: in the early evening sun, children chased each other, giggling with glee; young couples embraced, looking out to sea; tourists posed for photographs. It was impossible to picture this as a scene of carnage and terror. But for Signor Carlo, as with all those *Taorminesi* of his generation, the streets of Taormina would always be tinged with the painful memories of bleak, difficult times when it would have been impossible to imagine this bustling, carefree scene of plenty.

His gaze returned to me and, smiling, he continued.

'I had to find my family. I lived near, but it wasn't easy to get there from where we were. When people asked me where I lived, I'd say *'ntò vadduni* [down the big valley] and that is because when it rained, it created a torrent that at times flowed impetuously down to the bottom. I found my mother and grandfather. My grandfather was from Palermo, but at that time he lived with us. Thank God, they were completely unharmed.

'The house hadn't been touched by the bombs, as it was slightly off the planes' route, but just a hundred metres away, other buildings had been reduced to rubble. We had nowhere to go, so my father, who had also escaped injury, came to our aid, and all together we walked towards the countryside.

'We walked at night through country paths for more than five hours. The paths were full of people, fleeing in search of refuge. Our destination was I Pantani, a district where my father knew the Castagnas, a farming family he stayed with during his hunting trips. But it's one thing to host one or two hunters in normal times and an entirely different proposition to host a whole family during wartime, when there's not even enough for yourselves to eat. Your only hope is help from God.

'There were seven of us who called upon the hospitality of Signor Castagna that summer: my father, my mother, my grandfather Tommaso, myself, Donna Catena – who since the good times had taken care of my father's house and two of his children – as well as Turi and his sister Concita, who later became my wife. We stayed for about forty days in this remote place, forgotten by civilisation, and life was hard. The house had no water, no light, nor was there even enough space for us all to lie down during the night. Neither was there a toilet – you had to go behind the bushes. And there was so little food... Every day was a battle.

'The peasants who hosted us were poor, with barely enough for themselves, so we three men (my father and we two boys) – my grandfather was excluded as being too old – would head out into the countryside as soon as dawn broke. My father brought his hunting rifle. He had kept this secret, as it was forbidden to own one – whoever had any weapons was supposed to hand them in to the German authorities.

'We would set out, hoping to kill a rabbit or a partridge, and several times we returned with one of these spoils. But such small kills provide little more than a taster for seven people. So we would also scour the desolated countryside, its farmers called up to fight long ago, only to find a pear tree with shrivelled, unripe fruits or a vine that was no longer cared for but still produced a few grapes we could eat. This was our nourishment, coupled with cornflour, which we ground with two large stones rolled against each other using the strength of our arms.

'We would also seek out wild vegetables – of which Donna Catena was a great connoisseur – as well as baked chestnuts, carobs, dried figs, prickly pears and walnuts, which the farmers gave in small doses in exchange for a small fee. We gathered anything and everything we could find. This was our daily struggle.

'One day we managed to get some rice, thanks to Signor Campagna, a friend of my father and secretary of the municipality of Mongiuffi Melia. This rice came from the municipality of Letojanni, where fleeing Germans had abandoned a wagon with sacks of it. Soon the population found out, seized it and distributed it. Some of it ended up in this mountain village, where it was divided between several families, including that of Signor Campagna, who in turn gave a few pounds to us.

'About once a week, Turi and I returned to Taormina to try and get what we could with the ration card – four hours to get there and four hours back. They were quite pointless walks, as Taormina was deserted – especially the area of Cuseni. There was no water to drink and the heat was terrible. Several times I drank the stagnant water of a centenary well. The streets were heaps of rubble and the stench of corpses was everywhere… The dead were still under those piles of debris and were only later retrieved by the Americans.

'After weeks in the hills, we returned to Taormina, but it was difficult to live there. Many boys installed themselves in front of the hotels, where British and American soldiers lived. They were much more generous than the Germans. They gave us something to eat, and for the first time we saw crackers, canned cheese, corned beef, chewing gum and cigarettes. It was then that smuggling began – people were capable of getting hold of anything they could to resell. And Taormina was filled with improvised dance clubs. Nobody needed a permit – just a big enough room, two or three musicians from the old town band and drinks.

'The best liqueurs were found in Giarre – vermouth, sparkling wine made with bicarbonate… The military drank anything. Someone would collect the empty bottles and then sell them to a junk dealer, who passed by with a sack on his shoulders. Glasses were made by cutting in half bottles of beer, which the Americans consumed in large quantities. Everyone did whatever they could to survive.

'Some collected cigarette butts in the streets – the Americans threw them away only half smoked, though for us such a waste was inconceivable. Waiters in the dance halls collected butts left in the ashtrays, then resold them at a lower price. There were boys like us who sold loose American cigarettes in the street, carrying them in a wooden box attached to our neck… Everyone started to make their living again.

'The AM-lire – a new Allied Military currency – was introduced. And the first American aids brought us white flour, which was still rationed but so white it looked like a sort of sponge cake. Delicious.

'In a short time, dozens of girls, tired of starving in their villages, arrived in Taormina and began to prostitute themselves. The soldiers were full of cash. The girls went in the bars where all the soldiers drank and earned a lot of money, money they sent back to their families.

'When things settled and the Allies left, many of these girls stayed in Taormina and several had children – accidents of the trade. Others got married to local people. The descendants live in Taormina, and they pretend they don't know these dramas experienced by their mothers or grandmothers.

'I must say that there were no Taormina girls who prostituted themselves, except two very beautiful and well-known sisters and two of their cousins, who then married the soldiers and left with them for the Americas. I think the girls who came from outside the town would never have prostituted themselves in their own villages – both they and their families would be dishonoured for life.

'The town began to live again. The rubble was cleared and the corpses recovered. The streets were freed and people slowly began to repair their houses with what few means they had, recovering the material that lay at the edge of the streets. The trains started to travel but were crammed. Most of them were cattle wagons, and people clung on wherever they could – even over the roofs of the wagons. It was the only way to move from one place to another.

'Us boys discovered the great fun of disassembling abandoned cannon shells to recover ballistite – the explosive propellant in the ammunition. We put a thread, like a big piece of spaghetti, upside down under the shoe. It set itself on fire and ran away like a zigzag rocket between the legs of the frightened people. For us it was a good laugh!

'There were also small pieces of coloured silk inside the cannon shells that perhaps were used to keep the various powders separate. But for us they made beautiful belts.

'Now I think of the risk we were stupidly running, disassembling these bombs, because we had to slam them against walls to loosen the bullets from the cartridge case! The bombs were everywhere. Because of them, some people died and others remained disabled for the rest of their lives, but even so, nobody told us to stop…'

Signor Carlo trailed off, lost in his own thoughts as the ancient piazza echoed with the laughter and animated conversation of just another day. A day that was incomparable to what would have been, all those years ago. Different days, different problems, different solutions, of which Edward Cecil Page was but one.

25

Forgiveness

I typed away furiously, my jumbled thoughts gaining a new rational order. The moment the words hit my computer screen, they took a form they wouldn't take in my mind alone. The ground seemed to be moving beneath me, a life of certainties learned unravelling, slowly but surely. The enormity of the discoveries I was making was still, at that stage, just beyond my perception, but I already knew that things would never be the same again. It wasn't just that I was learning new and often unsettling things about my family's past, but also that I was having to reassess a lifetime of feelings for my father.

The counsellor I had started to see by this stage had told me that processing traumatic news and events would take time. This was something I was now learning to be true. She'd suggested writing everything down and it was proving to be a cathartic experience.

When I'd started this journey, I knew it wasn't going to be an easy one, but what I wasn't prepared for was the scale of the discoveries I was making. Nor had I expected there to be quite so much information readily available about Edward Cecil Page and my family's dealings with him.

There had been so much to deal with emotionally, and it was forcing me to rethink so much that I'd taken for granted. It was scary, daunting and at times unthinkable. Throughout my life, I'd seen my father as a selfish man, a terrible husband and an even more terrible father. A man who'd spent his life thinking about the needs of one person only: himself. Now here, in black and white, ready for anyone to read, was evidence that from the age of eleven he had quite probably been abused by a man, who had, in the eyes of the world, adopted him, unofficially or not.

To the locals, Cecil Page had been a wonderful and generous English gentleman, surely not someone who would mistreat a young boy. Now it was beginning to look like my father's marriage to my loving mother had probably been an arranged one, to deflect from the ugly truth. In this context, perhaps all of the money he'd received was not an inheritance as I'd long thought but instead compensation for having stolen something priceless: a young boy's innocence and dignity.

It was overwhelming to discover so much, so quickly. At first, I wasn't ready to comprehend it all, so I pushed it to the back of my mind. Or at least I tried. But in truth, I never stopped thinking about it during those days, and it was only through talking to people, trying to process it all that I began to move on. To consider the circumstances, the poverty, the desperation, the war, how different life was back then. Slowly, I began to come to my own conclusions.

Part of me wished Richard had never asked those questions and that I'd never embarked upon this journey, instead blissfully following the Sicilian way. But I also knew that only knowledge would give me the freedom to truly move on and leave the past in the past, as painful as it might have been.

The rain poured down in heavy sheets outside the window. Underneath the wet, grey sky, the garden was a thick mass of green, a world away from the sparse and arid land of home.

My thoughts drifted to little Erica and Oliver playing on the lawn a few days earlier, laughing without a care in the world. As much as I tried, I simply couldn't imagine them living the childhood my parents had. There was nothing that linked my children's life of comfort in damp England to the continual struggles that my parents' and Signor Carlo's generation had endured in the dusty streets of post-war Sicily. Nothing, that is, except for me.

It had taken some time for me to understand just how much effect Signor Carlo's story had had on me. It wasn't the story in itself but the way in which it gave me a sense of my parents' childhood that I'd never quite grasped before. Hearing his words, I'd almost felt as if I was inhabiting their world, if even for only the most fleeting of moments. I'd only been a little girl when my mother had told me her stories, the details fading as the years went by. I'd never quite appreciated the severity of those poverty-stricken days and still I couldn't begin to imagine what life must have been like.

Oliver threw a toy at my feet, laughing as I looked up in surprise. I smiled but my thoughts remained far away.

My conversation with Signor Carlo had left me with an uncomfortable sense of incompleteness. Perhaps naively, I'd expected some sort of closure from it, to walk away with clear answers and explanations that would neatly fill all the remaining gaps in my family's story. Instead, I was left with more questions than ever. At the very least, I thought I would get a clear sense of whether my father was more victim than beneficiary, but instead I was left with that very Sicilian sense of words carefully left unsaid.

If one thing was clear, it was that the people of Signor Carlo's generation understood that time as being one of difficult decisions, each and every day, just to survive. It was dawning on me that I was never going to have someone tell me definitively what my father's experience and motivations were. I was going to have to decide that for myself. At least I was beginning to gain enough knowledge to enable me to do so, though whether I actually wanted to entirely revise my opinion of my father I was still not sure.

The word 'lucky' peppered Signor Carlo's description of my father, but it left me feeling uncomfortable. *Lucky* was what

Erica and Oliver were; *lucky* was how I felt to have the life I was living. *Lucky* didn't feel like the appropriate word for describing the dynamic between my father and Edward Cecil Page. You had to do what you had to do to survive, but *lucky*? I knew I should be feeling sympathy for the unimaginably difficult situation in which my father had been thrust, but it still felt too early for me to have those kinds of feelings. A lifetime of neglect and absence of empathy still weighed heavily on me.

Everyone builds a version of the truth that suits them, that allows them to continue living with dignity, to simply keep going. But if that turns out to be completely false, the fallout can be devastating and knock you entirely off balance. This is where I found myself.

Of everything I'd taken for granted about my understanding of my father, only the starting point remained the same: the famished eleven-year-old boy, dressed in rags, who ran into Villa Sole so many years ago. But the man he became, well, now I was unsure how much of that was his true self or a mask he had learned to wear. A charming man, with a particular eye for beauty, effortlessly playing the role of a serial womaniser, blessed with an immense fortune, but who in the process lost his heart and his humanity.

I wondered whether that boy would have become the same person if he'd never entered Villa Sole. Was his selfishness truly who he was? How much of it was the result of what he might have experienced over those years?

I imagined my father saying, 'This is all mine – no one else's. I have earned every single penny and I paid an immeasurable price.' I wondered whether I could blame him for following the path he did, but I was still far from believing that I could forgive him. My mother had done so, and I'd never understood that. Now, though, I began to grasp just why she had.

Yet I was beginning to sense that forgiveness might be possible, all the more so because I had a young boy of my own. Before too long, Oliver would be the same age as my father would have been when he accepted Edward Cecil Page's *job*. I would find myself looking at Oliver with that thought in mind and my heart would break.

26

Goodbye

I had a dream. I was in Taormina, standing in Chiesa Madonna della Rocca, the exquisite little church where my parents were married many years ago. On this occasion, though, I was there for my father's funeral. Beside me, holding my hand, was Richard with our baby daughter Erica in his arms. At my other side were my brother Edoardo, his wife Federica and my niece Atena. Oliver had not yet been born.

Throughout the service I felt nothing, just as I hadn't on the day it had actually taken place, but as the procession of mourners moved to the graveside and my father's coffin was lowered into the ground, a wave of sadness swept over me. A feeling far from that of the day itself.

The emotion was so strong, I woke with a jolt.

As my eyes adjusted to the dark, I saw Richard sleeping soundly and reassuringly beside me. I smiled as I remind myself just how lucky I was to meet not just him but his entire family. A family that had given me such a different sense of family life than that which I'd grown up with. I'd found a real sense of belonging.

Sadly, Richard's grandmother Sheila passed away soon after Erica was born. Many years later, Chop died too, at the age of ninety-four. Nonetheless, I was happy that in the short time I knew her, Sheila was able to attend her first grandson's wedding and also meet Erica, her first great-grandchild. Both my children grew up with the most loving great-grandfather in Chop, and he in turn lived to see four of his six grandchildren marry and in turn meet nine great-grandchildren.

Every Christmas, every birthday – any occasion – is an opportunity for the O'Sullivan clan to get together and celebrate. I'm so glad Richard and I made the decision to move north to be part of all this. We made, and are still making, so many wonderful memories.

I feel particularly blessed to have been able to contribute to creating those happy memories for Chop and Sheila, and fortunate to have had many years to enjoy Chop's company and get to know him better. I also like to think that I made one of Chop's dreams come true twice, bringing him to Sicily on two separate trips in which special memories were made. I have a wonderful image of him sitting in the shade of the mandarin tree at Villa Sole, wearing his panama hat and sipping a cold beer with a contented smile on his face – another English gentleman staying at Villa Sole, as Edward Cecil Page had done many years beforehand.

I feel a pang, not just for Chop, but also for the unconditionally loving, supportive father I never had and am still probably grieving for. But importantly, I've now made my own peace with my father, thanks to this process and the people who helped me along the way – Richard, Signor Carlo, Oliver, my family, my counsellor and even Sir Timothy Berners-Lee, the computer scientist who invented the World Wide Web that enabled all those devastating discoveries!

But I had to confront my own past family life.

Sometimes, I still look at my Oliver and wonder, *Why were all those terrible things allowed to happen?*

I know the answer of course. It was all about survival. Even child abuse was acceptable in those poverty-stricken days. Emotionally, I've had to learn to manage my feelings about it.

After all, I have an answer, albeit an unsavoury one, as to why my father was never the father I wanted. It's unfortunate that the timing of my revelations meant that I never had the chance to raise the subject of Edward Cecil Page with my father or tell him what I knew. But then again, how could I? Everything would have been completely different, had I discovered the truth when he was still alive.

For his part, my father held his secret close, never giving anything away. Maybe he'd locked the shameful truth away from himself as much as he had from the outside world. I will never know. He took his tragic secret with him to the grave. Everybody who'd known about it and turned a discreet blind eye has probably done the same by now. Even Signor Carlo, one of the few people left who lived those difficult times, recently passed away. Who is left to tell the story except me?

There's still some part of me that naively hopes it didn't really happen. After all, only two people could ever know the definitive truth – my father and Edward Cecil Page. Perhaps now that I've told my story, it's time that I lay it to rest with its now long-gone protagonists. It's time for me to move forward, to write my own story. Because if all of this has taught me one thing, it's that we can't judge the events of the past through the eyes of the present.

Art by Chiara Curcuruto

Postscript

In real life, there is another ending to this story – which is part memoir, part fiction – where I am standing holding a baby boy in my arms at my father's bedside in Villa Sole.

Outside, the fierce Sicilian sun is blazing down incessantly on the parched brown hillsides of Taormina. Inside this small room though, all hint of daylight is banished by the shuttered door and window. The only sound to be heard is the steady ticking of an old clock. My father lies still and silent in the bed that has become his home in his recent, lonely late years. Any concept he had of a life outside these walls is long forgotten.

I could so easily have opened the window blind to give him a stunning view of Mount Etna's snow-capped peak, but it would have been pointless. His longing for such sights has long passed.

Then, suddenly, there is a small whimper from him.

'Who is this baby?' he asks as he slides in and out of consciousness, moving between the past and the present. 'Mamma?'

Just as he seems to realise who I am – Beatrice his daughter, not his mother – I take my cue. 'Papà, this is your grandson Oliver.'

They are my last words to him.

About the Author

Agnese Mulligan was born and raised in Sicily. In her early twenties she moved to London where she lived for fifteen years before moving to the English countryside where she currently lives with her husband and two children.

Although Agnese has lived longer in the UK than in Sicily, she will remain forever bound to the place of her birth, its culture, cuisine and people. These themes run throughout her first novel, *Under the Mandarin Tree*.

Printed in Great Britain
by Amazon

10528113R00120